For my father,
Tom Black, who left before I arrived.

And for all the children who didn't enjoy
the childhood they richly deserved.

Thanks...

To all at Guildhall Press for their professionalism, hard work and encouragement. To Damian Smyth and the Arts Council of Northern Ireland for their much-appreciated support. To Marilyn McLaughlin for her wonderful illustrations. And to you, dear reader, for taking the time to explore the world of Zoom-Zang-Alang!
I hope you enjoy the adventure.

1 MiRTH MATTERS

'She's got her dress on back-to-front!'

You see, that was the way it was: there was no way of telling beforehand. So, out of the blue, a sudden strike from nowhere caught us unawares and we were off, laughing to our hearts' content, belly giggles bubbling up through veins into the mind and onto faces. There was no refuge from it in body or soul. I mention "soul" here, because this was an added problem – for today, at least – because we were sitting in the midst of God's holy Mass.

'Stop laughing!'

It was a sunny Spring Sunday, the loveliest season of the year. My olders, brother Tom and sister Siobhan, and my unholy self, benamed Liam, had been ordered out to save our souls as Momsie and Dad – known to the good folk of Drummond Town as Mrs and Mr White – rested theirs with their weekly lie-on in bed.

'I can't!'

For now, though, we found we had to stand up just when we needed to tuck our heads down, and when we had to respond by the way of prayer just when we needed to keep our lips tightly sealed.

'We're going to be thrown out – look, he's staring at us!'

Unfortunately, too, sniggers had long since vanished from the three of us, and by now the whole of our upper frames filled and filled and filled with a blend of laughter so strong that had no way out . . . for the moment.

'No, he's not . . . He's cross-eyed, he's staring over there!'

So there we were, well-near bursting with an explosion of mirth that needed an exit. It was bad enough for me, sitting on the right-hand side of Siobhan. I only had the rise and fall of one shoulder to contend with. This was the same for Tom on the other side. Our poor sis didn't stand a chance. She was middled between two laughing hyenas in the making, and now her shoulders were rocking in time with us, so that we three disrespectfuls must have looked as if we were seated on a wonky pew.

'He's watching . . . both side-doors . . . at the same time!'

And the more we tried not to notice each other, the more we couldn't help but notice what was really going on with the priest's eyes. This meant we had to be extremely determined with our inner selves, but the difficulty here was trying not to breathe, in case it was the catalyst for an explosive outcome.

'I bet you he can read both pages of a book at the same time!'

There was, therefore, a little holy hole in the congregation, about three young persons wide, but not very thick, because the three of us were bent treble with the bubble of mirth, now overflowing out into the presence of looks returning from all around. Once you give a snigger any sort of a little start, it becomes impossible to stop, especially since the big, naked "V" of her dress, whoever she was, was slap, bang, wallop in front of our watering eyes, showing off the nakedness of a lot of freckly flesh.

What were we supposed to do?

How were we meant to stop?

Impossible!

All we could do was stand there and give vent to the enormous, unstoppable supply of laughter, because once the tiny trickle found its way out, the torrent behind very quickly followed. Each of us knew the volcano of the absurd inside was about to erupt. We had to go. Priestly cross-eyed glares or not.

'Excuse me!'

'Excuse me!'

'Excuse me!'

It was a very brave, or desperate, person indeed who would excuse themselves from the packed ranks of turning heads of Sunday's church congregation. However, the three of us couldn't hold it in any longer. We excused ourselves as we pushed through the tangle of legs and bodies and feet, making for the freedom of the aisle.

'Thank you!'

'Thank you!'

'Thank you!'

Off we dashed, out along an aisle and through the nearest side-exit, which burst open with our need. With three hands dipping heavily into the splash and hand-soak of the holy-water font in the small porch, we found our minds couldn't command our legs to respond quickly enough to help us escape from the alleluia chorus thriving in our wake.

'Alleluia, alleluia, alleluia . . .'

Just then, the full majesty of the sun's silvery shine emerged and the full glory of God's message was made known to us as a trio of laughter erupted from our insides. It was a sun-staringly beautiful moment in a glorious day and, in those few seconds, we were lost in its wonder.

'Alleluia, al-le-lu-ia!'

Even when we stepped down off the tiles of the small porch, we still couldn't talk, and we certainly couldn't help ourselves enough to make anything other than a very rubbery sign of the cross as we made our getaway.

'Aaahhh ha ha ha ha ha ha ha!!!'

'How could anyone be so stupid? I mean . . . put on a dress back-to-front . . . come on!'

It was Tom who first managed to squeeze just enough of a semblance of intelligence back into his system to allow for word formation.

'Maybe she's twisted!'

Before she even said it, I knew it was going to happen; I could see it in her eyes. I knew Siobhan was going to start the bubbly ball of laughter off again, rolling around our insides and squeezing out every spark of lively and happy and jocular and jocose still lurking within.

And so we were off – helpless. We were like wriggly worms washed onto the footpath after rain, except we were on grass. We ended up rolling about on the neat lawn, in the shadow of a curious but silent monkey puzzle tree, and there was no way we could stop ourselves laughing. We knew, inside our insides, we had the freedom to enjoy ourselves and each other, for now, in our paroxysms of mirth, and for a little while longer.

Enjoying a little laze on the lawn of life is wonderful, and it doesn't matter if this lasts for seconds, minutes, days or whatever. However, during our moments in

touch with the happiest of giddy selves soaking through us and into the grassiness thereunder, we probably enjoyed more of the goodness of life in that one silly morning than many poor souls can capture in a lifetime.

Today, this bright and sunny Sunday morning, it wasn't possible for most of the rest of the congregation still worshipping within to share in the absorption of life we felt all around. So we stayed a little while longer, after we'd thrown ourselves onto the giggles of our bellies to cook the other side of our laughter. It was brilliant. The freedom to let it all out – not having to hide it, to mask the look of something so natural, so funny, so wonderful – was the greatest of all reliefs.

Eventually we wound our way down, down, down from this elevation of highest feeling. Gathering our normal selves and quietened thoughts, we departed the scene of our hilarious escape and wandered off in a direction we knew only too well.

By now, though, all sorts of possibilities were pursuing new wants around inside our heads, and leaving us ready for whatever came next.

2 BAKER DAD

Sunday, it has to be said, was the only day of the week when we didn't rise to the powerful odour of freshly baked bread finding its welcome way into the house.

Mmmmhhmmm!

The smallest of gaps in windows provided open invitation for this healthiest of smells to sneak in and absorb us. Larger gaps under doors did their best to drag in as much of this fine smell as they could manage. Even the minutest of creaky gaps between floorboards did their uneven best to admit the smell of our family's success.

Yummylicious!

And since it arrived in the very early of every morning to explore how we were and how we were getting along, no corner escaped its notice, no nostril hair didn't curl up in appreciation, no mind wasn't captivated by the glory of its baking wonder.

Fantabulous!

Dad was a baker, a master-baker, to give him his proper title, and six of the seven mornings of every week, he rose early, went into his bakery at the side of the house, and baked. Baps and bread, freshly supplied, were the order of the day every day, except Sunday. Mind you, if it had been left up to the locals, they would have had him baking fresh breads for them on a Sunday, too.

'Don't give people what they want *all* the time. They'll forget they're being spoiled and think it's your duty to do for them. People like the notion of being spoiled; it wouldn't be right taking that away from them.' That was the way Dad saw things.

Every other day, though, Dad did spoil them. Monday, Wednesday and Friday, he baked them pastry – after the bread and baps had been delivered. Tuesday and Thursday it was cakes. What a treasure of a treat! For this is when our real dad could be seen and fully appreciated. This is when he came into his own as master-baker, chocolatier, and inventor of delicious edibles to the nice folk of Drummond Town and its ever-expanding environs.

New flavours, new recipes, new mixes and blends, were always being tried and tested and rarely found wanting with the good people of around and about. Whereas *all* Dad's new ideas were generally good, some were *very, very* good, and so these would be included in his range of baking until something better came along.

Normally, this came with the change in seasons. So, at Christmas time, the artist in Dad would go to town, literally, with beautifully iced depictions of a little catch of life somewhere hereabouts. Therefore, one set of cakes would show Pat the postman on his delivery round. Another showed Mike the milkman doing the necessary with milk bottles. But, everyone's favourite – the crowning glory of his year's work and the limited edition they all talked about and wanted so much – was the Sunday Scene. A great parade of people coming out of church was Dad's *pièce de résistance.*

Everyone wanted one. Everyone who could, had to have one to show off to everyone who didn't have one, for that's the way folk are; townsfolk, cityfolk, country-folk – it doesn't matter what they are or where they live, they're all made the same. And their reactions are no different, either.

'That's me there.'

'No, no, that's *me* there.'

'That's you there? No, no, that's you *there.*'

'Do you think so?'

'I know so. Look.'

'But I don't remember wearing red.'

'Oh, that doesn't matter. It's definitely you.'

We'd stand about, listening, taking in all that was being said about what was far from evident on any one of Dad's beautiful creations. And all the time we were thoroughly amused and amazed at what was going on in other people's minds.

'Don't put them off their notion. Money couldn't buy this sort of advertising,' is what Dad would say when we reported back to him what we had heard said.

But the goodly people of Drummond didn't need any encouragement from us.

'They're too good to eat.'

'It would be a sin to take a slice out of a work of art so beautiful.'

And they were right.

In the end, though, they couldn't resist; nobody normal could. It's just that the truth was slower to dawn on some than on others: that it would have been an even graver sin not to tuck in and enjoy even a small slice of Dad's masterful and marvellously delicious creations, and to share this enjoyment with as many others as generosity would allow, than to do nothing at all with it.

'Everything in life is there to be enjoyed. Make sure you don't miss out on what's good for you,' was Dad's advice to us.

At Halloween, Dad baked cakes shaped like pumpkins, and cakes and buns with all sorts of ugly witches' faces on them. Again, when sometimes we'd be with him, helping carry in deliveries, the constant wonder from passing shoppers was:

'They're absolutely wonderful, marvellous. How do you do it?'

No matter what way this question was asked of him, Dad always had the same answer up his rolled-up sleeve:

'Oh, it's dead easy.' And he'd smile a soft smile and walk on.

So, that's all we thought, that's all we knew, because that's all we thought we knew. But it was enough to be getting on with, and so we got on with what we wanted every day to be spiced with, which was little enjoyments like this.

The first real enjoyment of every day was tucking into a bowlful of Momsie's most delectable of creations, her own special blend of porridge à la secret chocolate mix only she herself knew. It had been a long time in the find but, once found, it was going to be held onto for our evermore because it simply made getting up every morning much more worthwhile. And so, with lips licked clean and bellies purring with delight, we were a match and more for anything that came our way in the day.

On schooldays this amounted to helping Dad load the baps and bread into the van for delivery to the shops here, there and further away than we ever would have tried for on our bicycles. But we were dropped off at school before Dad ventured off into the outlying districts. On exceptional days, when the school register didn't demand our presence, and after we had helped clean the bakery of all its white sootiness, we could set off with Dad on his magical delivery tour.

Although the shops we visited all seemed the same, with the same blend of people as customers, the way to and the journey from, never seemed to follow along the same route. It was as if we were always nearly somewhere when an idea with a difference popped into Dad's head and so the van then decided to head off in a direction entirely of its own.

'We haven't visited Jones's nailery this long time' or 'I think it's market day over in Sudsbury' were the kind of statements Dad was liable to come out with at a moment's notice.

And so we'd end up in a different world. In a world where the air was full of clanking sounds rising from the efforts of tough, hardened men with grimy faces, and tiny cigarette ends smoking off dry lips, as they hammered and trolleyed and lifted heavy loads. Or in a world where the air was full of heady smells, with hard working men behind grinny faces, puffing pipe tobacco smoke through the hold of ruddy red lips, while the poke of long sticks shifted the slowness of cattle or the nervousness of sheep. These were the people and places of all around and hereabouts, and Dad knew exactly when the best of them all would be on show.

What's more important and more to our point, they all knew Dad and were glad enough to see him, and gladder still to lighten his load for the road home. However he kept a note of it all I'll never know, but somehow Dad knew things about them, and sometimes this was evidenced in what he brought. It was really great to see the rise of surprise on an unsuspecting face.

'A birdie tells me your Jane has given birth. Well, here's a christening cake for her. I hope the boy's a mite better looking than that ugly bug she's married to.'

That was Dad, you see; he didn't hold back in the saying or doing of what he was thinking. People liked him for that, and they liked him all the more for the wonderful creations that rose up like magic from the dexterity of his hands.

He could say things to the hardiest of men, and get away with them, too, because they all had the measure of him. There were no hidden depths with Dad. In the nailery, the foundry, or any of the other noisy, thumping, metally places men from around and about had no option but to work in, as if by magic their hardened, rough, furrowed faces and shovelly hands, melted away. Then they became like Dad: young and happy and jokey within themselves and with each other.

This was the sort of magic Dad could work, the sort of magic he *did* work regularly, along with the magic he constantly worked. This was taste-bud magic. The magic of bite and chomp and mush and mash with teeth and tongue and every little bit of oneself every time one of his deliciousness of sweet creations found the shortest route from hand to mouth.

Eating one of Dad's pastry sensations wasn't just a delight to the sense of taste, or smell, or touch, or sight, or munch: it went a lot higher than that, a lot further than the sixth sense, intuition – which tells us a lot about ourselves and more about others. Dad's deliciousnesses went right up into the higher faculties of intellect and spirit, ticked all the right boxes in each, and tickled a few more besides.

'You might as well enjoy yourself with the fancy stuff. Just so long as you don't lose sight of the basics, for that's your bread and butter, it pays the bills. The rest is the icing on the cake.'

Therefore it was that from early every morn except Sunday, Dad was out in the bakery creating the fresh doughy appeal of bread and baps, the mainstay of his production line. The smile Dad wore, after delivering this oft-repeated surety of belief, sometimes led him off somewhere else inside his head, perhaps into a new challenge, a new recipe, another idea for something big, really big, something that was going to take his name away and far and restore the family to what he claimed was its rightful fortune. Even at night, when he should have been lost under the influence of a dark, heavy snooze, brightness would sparkle from his eyes, a smile would register on his lips, and off he would trot, out to the bakery of dreams, to try out a new something or other that tickled his fancy.

For a long time, off and on for almost a year, Dad was convinced chocolate was going to do it for us. We didn't mind this mini obsession of his in the slightest because we were his more-than-willing guinea pigs.

At the oddest times of day or night, sometimes even after we had all long been in bed and should have been fast asleep and far away inside our heads, Dad would invite us to get up and sample a little piece of this or a large chunk of that. Brilliant! Until Momsie got wind of what was going on and she'd chase Dad back out to the bakery with his experimental chocolate product, and the three of us were shooed into the bathroom to scrub all taste of sweetness off our teeth with the white, bright sweetness of toothpaste.

I don't know why it was but Dad never thought of doing anything ordinary. Never once would he even consider manufacturing a normal, run-of-the-mill, bar of chocolate. Oh no, it had to be created to the very best of his ability because Dad was convinced his would be no ordinary success story. Dad was seriously counting on success happening after God knows how many failures and I would even be so bold as to say that he relished the prospect of these failures almost as much as the lure of eventual success.

Our dad had himself well and truly convinced, and ourselves decreasingly so, that when success did happen to bloom in our beautiful household, it would be as a result of something amazing and different that had never been thought of before. According to Dad, if a product was ordinary and only worth mass-producing, it wasn't worth his while copying.

So, chocolate with bubbles in it, it was. Yes, we all knew this had been successfully marketed by a big chocolate firm somewhere out there. Dad's mind always managed to take him one step beyond, though. The bubbles in Dad's chocolate were to be filled with nitrous oxide, N_2O, otherwise known as laughing gas. You really do have to hand it to Dad: nobody else had a mind that would think this way – certainly nobody normal.

It was quite an exhilarating thought, and for months Dad tried and tried and tried different mixes to get the N_2O to blend properly into the chocolate. All to no avail. He failed delightfully. Momsie reckoned it was all the laughing that made him unable to concentrate fully and thus successfully complete his mission.

We did try a few bars Dad thought might have come through the process properly, and we sneaked a few more chunks of bubbly deliciousness into school with us, but it didn't have the desired effect, quite the opposite in fact. The samples we tried at home, well, we weren't really sure, and although we so wanted to say yes, yes, yes, and laugh, laugh, laugh, well, we couldn't sway our internals to do so.

In the end, we tried the best we could to laugh. We tried the best we could to smile. We tried as best we could to hide the fact that the taste was so awful, so terribly dreadful, so astoundingly disagreeable, we had to swallow it down as quickly as possible and then run like mad for the nearest loo.

Unfortunately for me, I must have had the greatest thole, and so I was able to control my reactions the longest, and therefore I was last of the three of us to flee. The unfortunate part here comes with the knowledge that there are only two loos in our house, one upstairs and one downstairs. No matter what way you try to recalculate it, three into two doesn't go, never has gone, and will never go. Tom had nabbed the upstairs loo, Siobhan the downstairs, and therefore for my only convenience I had to hot-tail it into the back garden and relieve myself near a fine patch of dock leaves, while thanking the merry heavens for them.

I immediately knew exactly to whom the remainder of this chunk of chocolate would be offered the following day at school. A very definite few unsavouries in class would have the especial privilege of Dad's gruesome concoction re-educating their posteriors.

Fortunately for them, as I inveigled myself into their company on the long meander to first lesson next day, I had my hand out, ready to offer the rear reactionary chocolate when I was caught.

'Right, I'll have this! You know the rule about eating between lessons: it'll ruin your concentration. Ha, ha! Bad luck, boy.'

In a very grand, whippish movement, the chunk of chocolate was snapped out of my hand by that greedy guts, Mrs Nottulg, who married a German because she couldn't find anyone silly enough over here. And off she triumphantly traipsed toward her classroom.

Not a word of objection was uttered by my lips.

In fact, *good enough for her* is the thought that ran through my mind, for she had more than a bit of a reputation for always being on the lookout for something to eat. Some said she went through their bags at break-time, sneaking out bags of crisps, taking what she wanted, and Sellotaping the remains down – half-empty, of course. This was the day she would get her comeuppance, and by morning break it was reported to me she had been out to the toilet no less than three times. By lunchtime, she was nowhere to be seen, having had to slip off home with the urgency of the mood that was in her.

After this laxative escapade with the bubbilicious splatter-effect of the N_2O, Dad decided to leave chocolate behind for a bit. And so he turned his attention toward a new challenge that had been bubbling away at the back of his mind for a long time: sweets. Sugary sweets, or, to tag them with their correct appellation according to Dad, boiled sweets.

No matter what the type of sweet, the basic recipe stayed the same; only the colouring and flavouring differed. Plenty of sugar was the main ingredient, with about one third again of glucose being added. Roughly an equal measure of water to glucose was poured in; 'pint to the pound' as Dad liked to say; 'litre to the kilogram' as we liked to correct him. This was followed by a dollop of citric acid powder. Dad knew what was what. He knew that carelessness or inefficiency on his part would result in "scrap", which is the trade term for what cannot be sold, and what we found was not only difficult to eat but also impossible to share with all but the most desperate of associates.

Therefore, at all points of the process, Dad paid strict attention to detail. He made sure his boiling pan was kept absolutely bright and sparklingly clean because the least speck of sugar crystal from a previous batch would result in "candying", leaving the product unfit for sale. This had an unfortunate side effect for us, too, because it meant our jaws were sore from so much biting and chewing, our teeth were bruised from such hard battling, and our tongues felt like they had gone ten rounds with the world's worst munch.

It was hardly surprising, then, that there was no disagreement when Dad insisted he alone amongst the whole family was allowed to clean the boiling pan; not even Momsie was regarded as being capable of providing the level of spick and span needed.

But still it didn't work out as it was meant to. As chief tasters, we reckoned plenty of Dad's sugary production was more than good enough for a bit of shelf life. But Dad wasn't having any of it, informing us knowingly:

'You're only tasting the sugar' or 'The glucose hasn't blended properly.'

There was always a reason for the end result to be deemed unsuitable for human consumption, not to mention unworthy of its proposed purpose. None of this could we see, because none of this could we taste, because our palates, our tongues, weren't educated enough for the wises of sweet production. Not even when it was pointed out by the keener internal eye of the expert's finely tuned taste buds could we see it, but this didn't stop us from agreeing with Dad.

Our disappointment was as nothing in comparison to Dad's. We knew he wasn't in it for the money; he wasn't like that, although Momsie often said there was plenty needing done if there was ever any extra going. We knew Dad was doing it for himself, to prove something to himself as well as to a few others, and yet it wasn't working for him.

'I think I should give up and buy a lollipop machine.'

We knew inside our heart of hearts Dad didn't really mean this, not fully, although I reckoned it might not have been the worst idea he ever came up with, but I kept this to myself. However, the morning after he gave up all prospect of ever becoming the boiled sweet expert of our part of the globe, Dad's change of heart was a bit too obvious and unreal for our liking.

'I think I'll become a potter, instead.' That was it. That was all he said.

We nearly swallowed our spoons along with the deliciousness of Momsie's chocolate porridge we were tucking into as usual for breakfast. The three of us sat there, spoons at the ready, waiting to see what was going to happen next.

'Don't be silly, dear.' Momsie didn't mince her words. Yet she knew she had to continue and say something a bit more encouraging, and perhaps also a tad more befitting our ears.

'You're good at what you do, darling. What makes you think you'd be good at anything else?' This time, there was a sight more encouragement in her look than in her words.

This set Dad's mind athinking, and his eyes off alooking somewhere out into the distance beyond the hold of our kitchen window. While his mind followed his eyes off into the beyond of our hold, Momsie whispered to us. 'I think your Dad's gone potty!'

We all had a good laugh at this. Dad, too, when he eventually managed to burst his way out of the little bubble he was in. Only then did it feel right to say our piece, and bring out into the open what the three of us had often discussed on our own.

'Dad, what about chewing gum?'

'Yes, Dad, you could make some brilliant chewing gum!'

'And bubble gum, too, Dad!'

'Different flavours instead of the boring mint and strawberry ones.'

'Yeah, you could have banana, pineapple . . .'

'Mango . . . and spices, too . . .'

'Spices?' Tom and my worried self reacted the same way to Siobhan's last addition. We then saw from the look on Dad's face that this might not have been the high-class end of confectionery he fancied cutting his angle into.

'Brilliant idea! That's a wonderful idea, and it's exactly what we're going to do next!'

Although Dad's words sounded real enough, we weren't so sure that his heart would be taken with such a basic product. We'd have to wait and see.

3 GUMMY GAMES

We didn't have too long to wait and see because, by the time we were home from school that very same day, Dad had the theory sorted on the principles of what made up a wonderful piece of chewing gum or bubble gum.

Unfortunately, that's as far as the exercise on chewing gum got, and it didn't leave the surface of the page the next day or the next or the next. One crucial ingredient was missing, and remained missing until the following week when Dad's suppliers took delivery of a sizeable load of gum chicle for him.

'Don't put that stuff anywhere near your mouth!' Dad knew me only too well. He noticed my greedy mit heading for the gummy whatever it was, and thence straight for my greedier gob. 'If you swallow any of that, we'll have to put you in Madame Tussauds because you'll clog up and stick together from the inside out!'

I immediately withdrew the reach of my hand. I had no wish to become a gummy dummy that looked nothing like me.

We were allowed to watch the making of the first batch, as the load of glucose was brought to the boil, and then the heat was reduced while the gum which was crushed into small pieces was gradually added, stirring constantly, and then cooked until it was melted and evenly incorporated. Dad let it settle off the heat for about ten minutes. Icing sugar was then stirred in, and in Dad's first batch, oil of spearmint was thoroughly mixed in; he thought it best to play safe with the flavours to begin with.

We were all allowed to help with the hard work process of dusting with icing sugar, kneading with the knack of our knuckles, flattening as best we could on whatever flattish surface came to hand to roll out to a proper chewing gum thickness. By this stage we all had our own piece to work on and I was rolling and turning, rolling and turning, with the help of a milk bottle.

'Can we try a bit now, Dad?' To my mind, there should have been some immediate reward for such pressing, hard work.

'No!'

'Please, Dad!' Siobhan's supplication emanated more from the flutter of her eyelashes than the petition of her words.

'No.'

'It would do no harm to test the flavour of its consistency.' Tom smiled hopefully. He needn't have bothered.

'No . . . Tomorrow.'

Although we three youngers were salivating at the prospect of masticating our way through a block that was all of our own make, Dad wouldn't allow. We had to leave what we were working on so it could be marked out for cutting the next day. Only then would it be ready to be broken up into pieces and wrapped in waxed or greaseproof paper. And next day couldn't come quickly enough for us.

Despite our inklings that we couldn't possibly last twelve hours without tasting and enjoying the absolute deliciousness of our own creation, almost, we did wait, simply because we had to. Dad's word had made it plain, clear and obvious there was no choice in this matter. Furthermore, we didn't just last the requisite twelve hours Dad had originally inflicted on us, but a full twenty-four hours in total to be exact.

Dad being Dad, in aftermath he had decided to add another few flavours to his chewing gum collection and he also manufactured a bubble gum range for the added entertainment of our lungs. We were very far from being disappointed.

The chewing gum range, like its bubble gum counterpart, had four flavours: spearmint, strawberry, banana and, of course, liquorice, for Dad's own liking. As master-tasters, we started off with spearmint chewing gum, moved onto strawberry bubble gum, enjoyed the momentous taste sensation of banana chewing gum, before being finished off by liquorice bubble gum. The reaction was almost immediate, but I must have been slightly ahead of Siobhan and Tom in the chewing process because I was first off the mark to book my seat on the downstairs loo. I had no care for which of the other two gained a controlling interest in the upstairs lavatory, I was much too busy with my own concerns.

Poor Tom. I ignored his hammerings and clamourings, his pleadings about his needing.

'Not in my herb garden!' Momsie's roar through, and rattle on, the kitchen window proved futile. Tom must have been a split second ahead of her and, as everyone knows, once you've let yourself go, there's no going back.

By the time the three of us were ready for bed that same evening, we were well cleaned out. And after the unending tirade of abuse led off by Momsie – but added to in no short measure by our empty selves – the house was filled with the unremitting sound of apologies from Dad. He had obviously added a bit too much liquorice to his mix. And this gave me a brainwave.

Next day at school, although I held out a hand clearly showing off an item of immediate edibleness, Mrs Nottulg quick-stepped past me, her nose up to the poke of the air, muttering away at sounds indistinguishable as words except perhaps to those with an aural ability in another language. At least she had learnt her lesson.

Before class, I made sure anyone who wanted some received as much as I deemed would be good for him from my ample supply of bubble gum, liquorice flavoured of course.

Roddy Redman was first. Although no one would say it to his face, everyone knew he was a positive definite for the world title of dumbest person on earth, if anyone was ever stupid enough to award this award. This was the one and only redeeming feature about him, which is quite something in comparison to the rump of scallywags and ne'er-do-wells he dwindled away the hours of his life with. Four of these sorts were very quick in their haste to accommodate their stricken backsides on the seated rescue of cubicles around Roddy Redman. The blasts and blows were of such an intensity that half the school thought the wind section of the orchestra was warming up for a performance.

'Jeez, that's great stuff, White! Got any more?'

Not quite the reaction I had anticipated . . . but, of course, I had; who was I to deny them their birthright?

By mid-morning my head was dropped right down upon my desk, as if I was trying to smell the grain of the wood thereunder. I was, in fact, trying to hide my face from seeing or being seen. A couple of Roddy Redman's numbskull acquaintances had managed to blow bubbles into their bubble gum, and to keep blowing, and keep blowing, until something akin to the size and shape of a balloon, stretched out in front of their eyes. It was only a matter of time.

'What on earth are you two doing?'

Even Miss Sunnyhuckle, our normally pleasant but slightly absent-minded teacher, couldn't miss out on the sniggers awakening her to the fact that something was obviously awry with her class.

Now it was all right for all of us to have a good giggle and goggle at Durks and Turps – Dick Durkin and Tobias Turpin – who had been quietly engaged in a private competition of the sort that wanted to see who could blow the biggest bubble. To the rest of the class the real buzz of excitement came from the wonder as to which head was most likely to blow up first, after the unrelenting, exhaling efforts of their own inflation.

It was obvious to all but one in the classroom that they couldn't answer. Therefore, Miss Sunnyhuckle reiterated her question, only this time a bit more loudly.

'What on earth do you two think you are doing?'

It was immediately clear to the rest of the class that Durks and Turps didn't know what to do, which was probably just their normal reaction to everything anyway. And it was massively clear and obvious to the vast bulk of our gathering that the said two would never, ever, not in a million years, know how to extract themselves from a situation such as this. They needed help. Now!

'Please, Miss, I don't think they're in a position to talk. I think they should go outside before they explode. It could be very messy.'

I liked the bit I added on at the end, but now Miss Sunnyhuckle was staring directly at me. I smiled. I knew this always eased the tension for those who did not or could not understand a given situation. Silence ensued.

'I'll take them out, then, shall I?'

I knew enough to know not to wait to give an undecided person the chance to make the wrong decision. And when I was up leading the two balloon gummers out and away at a safe distance for myself, but not for those around, she still hadn't managed to squeeze even the hint of a response from her statued frame.

The two twits didn't argue either, at least they had enough sense to know when someone was doing them a good turn, or not; and for some other reason they may even have believed I was the person with the gumption to see them out of their ordeal. So, as soon as our six feet rested fairly and squarely on the no-man's land of the corridor, I turned them to face each other, and gave the back of their heads a good, firm slap.

BABANG!!

The double bang that ripped through the air was of enough magnitude to induce a light roar of approval from a couple of classrooms on either side. Unfortunately for Durks and Turps, their faces were bespattered, besplotted and bespludged by the sticky remains of liquorice bubble gum as it stuck tightly to the soft skin of their freckly faces.

'If I were you two, which I'm not, thank God, I'd spend the rest of the morning in the toilets, picking off as much sticky goo as possible.'

And I thought to myself that at least now they were in possession of something to chew on, and a bit tastier than was their normal pick at the front of their faces. With that, I left them to do their worst with themselves, preferring instead the erstwhile comfort of my own chair at a shared desk.

'It'll take them a while to pick the stick off their faces, Miss.'

Miss Sunnyhuckle only interrupted her reading for long enough to smile back at my words rather than at me; she was obviously coming to an interesting point because I hardly had time to turn round before she was off again, blending her own inimitable sound into the words on the page.

I brought out a nice cheery grin, which I thought was useful for just this sort of occasion, and meted it out round the rest of the class. A little nod in the right direction I saved for Roddy Redman, who responded in kind with the production of a darkish bubble of gum, of not too inconsiderable a size.

Therefore, I had established two important facts about Dad's liquorice bubble gum, and they were positioned at either end of the disposal of flatulence. The one holding greater interest was the upper end, and more particularly, the making of great, big, bubbilicious balloons from it.

As soon as I shared this information with Tom on the way home from school, we got stuck into chewing and bubbling and blowing massive mouthfuls of strawberry and spearmint and banana, but to no avail. None of these, either singularly or combined, had the elasticity of intent of the liquorice. Just our luck!

So we had to start into the liquorice. To try and ease the consequence of the one major side effect here, we tried not to swallow, preferring instead to spit, spit, spit, as much of the noxious saliva from our gobs as was humanly possible.

In the end, Tom and my windy self were able to blow, blow, blow, the biggest balloony bubbles we had ever managed. As soon as we had them up to what to all intents and purposes looked like an enormous stretch, to the full of their contain, and right at the point where everything inside your head tells you they're going to burst, we popped the remainder of the gum from our mouths, quickly squeezing the end together so as not to let any air escape.

As I did this, I automatically felt the rise of my right arm follow through with the rise of the balloon. Soon, I was at full stretch, feeling that if I allowed myself a tiny jump, I would most surely begin to float up through the air. I gave it a go. It didn't work. I landed straight back down on the ground. Still, I knew there was something there, definitely a remarkable lightness, airiness and floatiness to the balloon.

Then I thought to myself the lightness must be in my head and it must have been caused by my body being unable to absorb so much liquorice so quickly. For I remembered once having read about dizziness being caused by eating too much liquorice over a sustained period of time. This must be something similar. So, I looked over at Tom.

Lo and behold, Tom was doing the exact same as me. I must have been right after all because it was too much of a coincidence for the two of us to be going bonkers at the exact same time. The same look of *this is going to work* was in his eyes. He must definitely have felt what I had felt to have responded in the same way as me. He wasn't having much luck in the take-off stakes either, though.

'Lend me yours a moment till I try something.'

Seconds later and my reach came upon the sticky end of the stretch of Tom's gummy liquorice balloon. As soon as he let go of his end, I could feel an incredible lightness of being fill me. Off I ran, down through the garden, striding into great big airy leaps as I did so. I felt like an Olympic long jumper, only in slow motion, as my kicking feet furiously paddled the air until landing six or seven metres away from lift-off. It mattered little to me that I was helped in this fact by running downhill all the way.

'Yipppeeee!'

I heard the sound rip through the air and I knew it wasn't coming from me because I was scared stiff doing what I was doing in case I suddenly took off for the upper reaches of the heavens above. Only now was I becoming conscious of Tom's screeches and cries of delight, as I left the downward containment of the garden and bounced into the great open freeness of the field beyond.

By now I had altered the aspect of my manoeuvre into a triple jump type effect, only longer, much, much longer. Then, when we neared the bottom of the field, Tom had to grab hold of me to make me stop, which I managed to do just before the spiky ends of a hawthorn hedge would have had me.

'It's my turn. Come on, let me have a go!'

In the time it takes to bald half a daisy, Tom was three-quarters the way back up the hill and he was going for it, I mean, he was really going for it. He wasn't jumping – he was bounding and bouncing his way back down and this he managed in about half a dozen landings in comparison to at least a dozen by me.

'This is greeeeaaaaattt!! Fantastico!! I'm flying without wings!'

This last bit he tried to sing, which might have had a deflationary effect on the two balloons because, by the time he was back down beside me, they looked well and truly knackered. And just then, too, one of the balloons took off out of his hand and up into the nothingness of the air above, but only until a gust of wind slapped it downward and into the mangle of the hedge.

Whatever remains of life were still left in the balloon, the hawthorn soon made mincemeat of, and it was a sad and sorry shrivelled mess of its former glorious self. One moment, a lovely big fat happy balloon of gummy origins, next moment, it looked as if it had come out the successful end of a starvation diet. It was a miserable, pathetic, shrinking, shrivelling contraction of its former fullness of self.

Then, taking a few steps backwards, Tom released his grip on the other bubbly balloon. Up, up, up, and away, away, away, it flew off to greet its new life up in the great, vast beyondness of the sky above, until it disappeared completely from sight.

'We should have attached our name and address onto it somehow, so whoever finds it could contact and tell us how far it flew.' Tom's mind was away off with his eyes after the line of flight of the liquorice-flavoured balloon.

'You mean, like a message in a balloon?'

I looked brightly at Tom to see if he would catch the line of my enquiry. He didn't. It was at times like this, therefore, that I felt it my duty to bring my brother's fantastical thoughts back down and onto *terra firma* where they belonged.

'Or it might reach the village, snag on some old biddy's nice clean washing, destroying her Sunday best, and have her on our doorstep within the hour waiting for Momsie to reimburse her the cost of a dry-cleaning bill. No, thank you very much!'

Tom stared back at me. He obviously didn't have my level of intent because he would have thought the situation through properly. I stared back. I knew he knew this was much the more likely outcome given our recent track record in getting the implausible to do the impossible.

'We'll have to think up a way of keeping tabs on the next one.'

From the look in his eyes, I knew Tom had his thinking cap on now.

'Right, sure you work on that, then.'

I knew my own mind wasn't much help in practical applications such as this. I was more than happy to leave this to the expert. On the wander back up to the house, we made our plans. And as soon as we were back inside it was straight over to Dad to see if we could strike a deal.

'Dad, the rest of the bubble gum, the liquorice gum, can we take it off your hands? You see, we've got an idea . . .'

'Take the lot with you. I'm done with chewing gum, bubble gum, any sort of gum. Toffee! That's what's going to make us our money. Simple! I don't know why I didn't think of it before.'

Although he had been lying in a semi-dozy state on the settee, Dad's eyes lit up and his mind burst into life as he pulled himself up with thoughts of toffee!

'There'll not be a tooth left in the house by the time you strike it rich with your ideas. We'll need the fortune to pay the dentist bills!' Momsie worked around Dad with her words, as well as finding the need to shift him about a bit so she could plump up the cushions, with heavy thumps from the palms of her hands. I felt sorry for the poor cushions, the way she was going at them.

Dad was too far away to notice this burst of over-anxious activity from Momsie, even though he was still seated on the settee, sitting up now, directing his thoughts out into the open.

'Yes. Toffees and caramels. Hard and chewy, soft and blendy. I'll have to work on my boiling points, sugar blends, emulsification of fats . . . yeah, that's the real secret of success. A full flavoured salt-butter, heated with the sugars, will give the best empyreumatic flavours. Oh, I can see it all now. I can smell it all now. I can taste it all now. I'm going to have to work long and hard on this one!'

Dad was in his element. Standing up now, pacing around, his slow deliberate strides leading him off toward his beloved bakery, the theatre of his dreams as well as the manufactory of his work. Once stirred, his thoughts and processes had begun their long, drawn-out route toward complete emulsification, and hopefully not overcaramelisation.

While Momsie's head took control of her thoughts and shook out their meaning, Tom and my awkward self began the slow, dignified parade out after Dad to relieve him of the burden of all that chewing and bubble gum.

We couldn't wait to get stuck in!

4 MAGIC WORDS

Over the following days and weeks, quite a pretty sum of cash was built up by the sale of all and every bit of gum in our possession, excluding the liquorice bubble gum, of course. It stayed put in a box under my bed, while the money collected was nearly the full of a long discarded piggy bank, now brought back into active service, which was stashed on top of our wardrobe.

As our haul of cash grew, so did our plans for it, for we decided this would pay for any and all production costs accrued with the planning, design and manufacturing expenses accompanying our great expectations for the liquorice bubble gum.

The exact nature of our conjectulations we were as yet unable to certify. There was still such a quantity of them and they didn't really amount to very much in their own right, but we were sure, almost sure, that from them there could only come something wonderful and fantastic. In other words, we knew what we wanted to accomplish but we also knew we didn't know how to accomplish what we wanted. Simple!

Every night after homeworks and study, every day during free periods, break and lunch, lovely white and empty sheets of paper we paraded before our eyes, and we sat, pen and pencil at the ready, waiting for that burst of inspiration to crack open the little bit of genius we needed to spark from our skulls. And so we waited and waited, and we waited and waited and waited.

Doodles were the most I ever managed, and Tom's lack of inspiration must have been pretty similar because not once did he show me a dot, not a circle, not a square, not a theory, not a phrase, not a line, not a word, not an exclamation mark, not even a question mark. Nothing. We were going to have to do better and we knew it. In fact, we were in dire need of doing something. Anything!

'You have to hand it to Dad, he never stops.'

Tom broke the spell of our two selves standing, silenced, awaiting divine inspiration, for we had almost given up all hope of ever cracking the code of brilliance by ourselves. Dad was toing and froing, in and out of his bakery, carrying, lifting, moving, stirring, checking, sampling, emptying, and starting all over again. And all this time his whistling didn't stop blending a wonderful mix of song and hope through the whole house, all the way in from his bakery workshop next door. And all this time in his ins and outs, he didn't stop smiling to himself, or spreading his smile onto all he came into contact with.

'I found it!' At last, my eureka moment seemed to have arrived: 'I know now what we're doing wrong!'

I could see my words lifted a great spread of hope onto Tom's face, and he couldn't wait for me to follow through with the remainder of what I had to say. I paused, but only for a moment. 'We're doing nothing when we should be doing something!'

The brightness of my shining face reflected poorly off Tom's immediate and obvious sense of disappointment. It was blatantly clear I needed to say more, and quickly.

'No, I mean, we have to *do* something. We have to get practical instead of trying to be technical on paper. A practical solution to a practical problem. A financial solution to a financial problem. A . . .'

At least Tom could see what I was going on about because he joined in this last bit which was a direct quotation from Momsie; in fact, it was a phrase she could blend to her own angle whenever she felt like it – '. . . a smelly solution to a smelly problem' or '. . . a communication solution to a communication problem', and so on.

'Let's get chewing!'

With our joint response, we were fighting through each other to see who could get upstairs and into the bedroom first to dole out the liquorice bubble gum.

It's hard work chewing to order, even when the order is your own and the chewing involves greater than normal amounts of gum, accompanied by longer than normal spells sitting on the toilet. There had to be an easier way; of course there had to be an easier way, but there wasn't.

Our jaws were sore from chewing, our lungs were deflated from blowing, our faces felt as if they were permanently deformed from the torture of so much pressure on the cheeks. And still we had to continue doing what we were doing: try, try, trying to get that bit more lift-off with that bit of extra dimension added to the gummy balloons that were eventually taking shape from the distortion of our mouths.

It was very definitely very determined work, and Tom and my deflated self duplicated each other with the effort we put in, which was easy to gauge by the size of the outcome. We were obviously well matched in terms of lung capacity because the liquorice balloons of our inflation were the exact measure of each other, twinned beyond compare.

But, as they grew, so, too, did our problem of what to do with them when complete, and this was the problem we couldn't see round. Hardly surprising, though, considering our minds felt as full as the balloons we had emptied all our energies into.

So, there we were, sitting in the garage, puffed out, trying to drag air back into our lungs, trying also to come up with a thought that would release us from the bind of stupidity we seemed to be in. The sealed balloons bobbed up and down in front of us inside their makeshift cage of scrap-wire fencing that Tom had uncovered.

'That was a bit of a wasted effort.' I don't know why I felt I needed to state the obvious.

There was no reaction from Tom. He didn't make a judgment on my lack of thought, or perhaps his silence did state a lot more than mere words could do.

We could feel from within that time wasn't on our side. We knew time was on the side of the call from the kitchen, pulling us away from what we weren't doing and back in to help prepare for the evening meal. We knew this meant that by the time we made it back out into the garage, all things going our way, the balloons would have given up their playful bobbing about and imploded onto the garage floor, meaning we'd have a whole mess to clean up.

'Right, let's get rid of these.'

It wasn't my turn to speak, and anyway, since Tom took the lead on this, I was prepared to go along with whatever. We were both long enough in the tooth to know that when you don't have a positive at hand, make sure you don't wait until you're stuck with a negative.

'Here, you take yours and I'll take mine.' On second thoughts, I thought it better to suggest something rather than be lumbered with them both.

A little less than a nod, a little more than a look later, and we were off outdoors together, looking a bit like boys we must once have been but couldn't remember, balloons in hand, on the lookout for fun.

'I'll dispose of mine first.'

We were only just round the corner from the house and I was determined to let go of mine as soon as possible and certainly before it became too clingy to my hand. I set it free, up, up into the vast airiness of the bright above.

Disaster!

I had been a bit too quick in the "let go" department and hadn't thought about what was barely visible but was still definitely there, up above, for my wayward balloon had decided to attach itself to the telephone wire connecting us to the rest of the talking world.

'Sugar! That wasn't meant to happen.'

This was all I could say because it was all I could think because I didn't know what was going to happen next, although I did hope it would free itself immediately.

Tom and my worried self passed one of those looks between us. We didn't know what would happen next, but, knowing our luck of late, the balloon would probably explode with all the electrical impulses passing so quickly through this long thin wire. Because at this time of day the wire was bound to be red hot with Siobhan chatting to all the friends she had only just left after school.

This was some sort of ritual girls put each other through, where they spent ages on the phone talking about what they had only just done. It wasn't as if anything wonderful and life changing had happened in between times. It wasn't as if they had suddenly discovered the theory of relativity; undiscovered it would have been more likely. Strange creatures, teenage girls are.

'Look!'

Tom's call swung my eyes back round to outward focus as I stared toward him to see what he was on about. I followed along the point of his arm and off the poke of his peter-pointer. I couldn't believe what I was seeing. It was all a bit hazy, a bit disturbed in places, not as clear and concise as eyes would have been used to but it was all there and happening in front of our eyes.

I know it's difficult to believe but words were appearing on the balloon. Call me delusional, call the two of us whatever you want, but there, up there, in front of our eyes, letters making up words were appearing more on than in the balloon; like magic.

But these weren't just any old words, oh no, they

were silly, stupid, rubbishy words strung together in a kind of a way that didn't make sense; gobbledegook. The more I stared and studied these changing forms of words, the less I understood what was being written because . . . because it was girl-speak.

This girly-talk was showing its embarrassing self to the watching world below. Not just any girly-talk but girly-talk of a very distinct disposition because it was what passed for a conversation between Siobhan and one of her pals. Girls' thoughts were compressed into this small language of words we were seeing and reading, but not necessarily understanding, and as they passed along the enormous length of telephone line, somehow they were messaged out to us on the liquorice balloon. Amazing!

It was either Mandy or Wendy that Siobhan was talking to, because, as far as Tom and my eagle-eyed self could make out, these were the only two names that hadn't yet come up in conversation. We were both trying as best we could, studying and concentrating really hard, but a lot of what was being said was coming out in two directions at once, which made it impossible to manage. What we really needed was another teenage girl who could translate and decipher at the same time.

Increasingly, the wording became less and less clear, more and more difficult to read as contact between balloon and phone line began to break. However, the greatest difficulty we were having with it all was because we could still hardly believe what we were seeing. Inside our own minds, something found it difficult to absorb what our eyes had tuned into and were showing to be true. We were totally unprepared for what we saw, not to mention our complete lack of understanding of how this was actually happening, when—

POP!!!

All sense of life, all transmission of talk, or chat, or whatever it was, expired from the gummy balloon, and it slapped in a sticky mess on the ground before us.

Almost as an automatic reflex, Tom angled his arm out and let go of his balloon, to the reckon of his aim and for it, too, to catch on the telephone line. Up, slowly, it headed toward its target, only to go seriously offline when it got near, and then it took off into the wide blue yonder of above.

'That was amazing!'

'Amazing? It was scaryspookyhallucinafreakyeerie-weird!! Wait till Dad hears about this, he'll laugh his

leg off!' I made to leave, expecting Tom to move at a double-quick pace with me.

'Hold on a minute.'

I stalled, more from the sound of Tom's deliver than from the actual words themselves.

'Let's think about this . . .'

Tom's stall here was perhaps to pick up on any signals I was sending back. My face brightened in anticipation of whatever was coming next.

'Why don't we work on this a while? We'll see if we can improve on what we've already got. We might be able to add another dimension onto what we have here.' There was a very positive little nod from Tom as he finished his words.

I hadn't a clue what he was talking about, and I reckoned the same was true for him, too, but what the heck! It was very definitely my turn to speak. I didn't know what else to say and so it was best I went along with whatever.

'Okay. Let's have a go!'

The next few minutes were spent picking up the fallen remains of our erstwhile readable balloon, and these remains we discarded in the bin. But first of all we checked the surface to see if there was any lasting imprint of the messages so recently displayed to us.

Nothing. Not a letter, not a mark, not a single, solitary sign of the fantastic experience Tom and my unbelieving self had been part of. Just gooey, glumpy, splunks of darkly faded bubble gum.

With mixed thoughts, we left the scene of our amazing discovery and headed indoors for sustenance.

5 GASSY IDEA

Inside the house, we very quickly reverted to normal, or what in our case passed for normal, as we helped in finalising the preparations for dinner. It's funny how your head can be full of the most extravagant thoughts one moment and then completely blank the next while your body indulges your spirit in the most mundane of household chores.

And soon, great lengths of spaghetti were twirling their way onto our forks and slipping and sliding down the fall of our throats and into the full of our bellies. Spaghetti Bolognese, how delicious! Especially when mopped up and helped down by plugs of Dad's crusty bread, shapes and ends a bit too crushed or misshapen for public purchase.

'Dad.'

A long slucking noise followed on from Siobhan's attention-grabbing sound bite. And now the mastication of many mouths stood on standby as we waited to hear what she was going to share with us. It was moments later when she decided to reacquaint herself, and the rest of us, with the challenge of slurping spaghetti and talking, both at the same time.

'Dad.'

A bit less announcement fed out from this one but, nonetheless, all ears were perked and attending on what was to follow. Dad's fork fell down onto its at-rest position at the side of his plate, while his eyes tried to measure up to the challenge of enticing whatever it was she had to say from her.

'Dad.'

We were all praying for third time lucky, either this or the spaghetti was going to have to worm its way onto all our forks on its own, so unamusingly intrigued were we by her laconic attitude.

'When I was on the phone to Wendy, she phoned me, of course, well she's always phoning, I don't know when she gets time to study . . .'

Here, Siobhan caught the look of Tom and my irritated self having a go at whatever she was rattling on about. The dirty look that came back from her was priceless; well, it was to us, for we certainly wouldn't have paid a penny to see it.

'There was a lot of interference on the line for a while. But it was all right again after I hit the receiver a few times against the wall.'

Tom and my mortified self had suddenly taken on the facial appearance of two big overripe tomatoes. As Siobhan's head fell back down to the challenge of her dinner-plate, Dad smiled, a dry, wry looking grin.

'Try tapping it against your head the next time.' I knew this was what he was thinking and I thought I'd help him out a bit by offering up the right message for consideration.

'That's enough of that . . .' And Dad was looking at me when he said this, imagine! 'It's probably only interference of some sort on the line. No need to take it out on the receiver.' It was very definitely a wry smile that followed on from the finish of his words, but he was looking at me this time.

'Who's this Freddy fella you and Mandy were yapping about? Does he do a lot of "care in the community"?' Tom had it out before I had a chance to kick him under the table.

'Daddy, it's not fair! They're always listening in to my private conversations!' Siobhan made the slight error of judgment of letting her knife and fork slam down onto her plate.

'Hey! That's no way to treat your fork and knife!'

I hoped my little play on words might lift the situation off the angle it was presently on and back to where it could do us no damage. And I still managed to catch Tom's shin with the toe of an outstretched shoe.

As eyes met and matched eyes, and followed the flow of looks around the table, a considered silence held sway over thoughts, but not for long.

'Eat your dinner while it's still warm. It doesn't do to eat hot food when it's cold, just as it doesn't do to listen in to the words of others that are no business of yours. You might end up finding out something you've no need to know.'

It was a general order for all, and a specific piece of

advice for some, from Momsie, who then added, 'What's this Freddy boy's surname?'

The smile from Momsie soon quelled Siobhan's look of wanting to be enraged, and we almost settled back into the feel of a family at one with itself at mealtime. But I just couldn't help myself.

'Listening in to other people's conversations? That's terrible!'

A haughty pile of pious majesty suggested itself on my face. I had to pretend to chew hard and try not to swallow to keep my smiles at bay. Momsie, Dad and Siobhan stared over in my direction, trying to second-guess whether or not I was being for real. Tom didn't bother even pretending to look my way. He didn't need to. Instead, he landed a cracking wallop from the slam of one of his toes on my right knee.

So unexpected was this, it almost shocked a curse out of my system, but I managed to refrain from expletives and instead winced into myself. All I could do was to pass an obsequious looking smile back Tom's way.

In fact, the truth of our remarkable discovery with the liquorice bubble gum balloon felt as if it was bursting forth from every look making contact with us, every glance seeming to meet with a knowing cast of the eye back at us.

How could the rest of them not see? How could they not know? Were they pretending? Couldn't they see from our smiling, happy faces that we had made one of the most startling discoveries of the age? Couldn't they see what this meant for the future of communication for a start?

I got lost in this last thought for a moment. I could see now our brilliant discovery mightn't be the best possible invention for the telecommunications network. And all of a sudden I could only think of the harm this might do in terms of listening in to, or watching into, or reading into, other people's conversations.

Come to think of it, what good could possibly come from this?

None.

What bad could possibly come from this?

A lot.

Later on, I passed these thoughts on to Tom. He considered them for a moment, agreed with me I was one hundred per cent right, and then announced quietly but confidently, 'I have an idea . . .'

In the history of all great disasters since time began, I suspect that, on occasions like this, most, if not all, were preceded with these same four – seemingly problem-solving yet ultimately grief-resulting – brief words.

But, like the bunny in the beams, I awaited the outcome with fatalistic curiosity.

'There's still some N_2O left in the cylinder. We'll try inflating our next balloon with it. It could work well for clarity of writing.' Tom's face was full of smiley wonder.

'What?' I couldn't believe my ears. 'Do you think that's wise? It might end up exploding and blowing our heads off, and maybe half the house as well!'

'Don't be silly. It'll be fine.'

Neither Tom's words nor the sound quality of his voice did anything to reassure me. Although he was a year ahead of me at school, I couldn't imagine him having learned so much in either physics or chemistry about the reactions of a gas such as nitrous oxide. I'd need to scrutinise next year's syllabus to ascertain for sure exactly what was what.

In the meantime, though, I knew I'd have to go along with big brother's assertion and hope and pray it would all turn out as I guessed he said it would – or perhaps this should be he guessed and said it would. Somehow, though, I had a strange feeling inside that told me we were biting off a bit more than we could chew.

The next couple of days were spent, when freedom of time allowed, laughingly trying to inflate a too-well-chewed, and quite slabbery, wet mass of liquorice bubble gum with N_2O. But it wasn't possible – certainly not without the ridiculous reducing influence of gas masks.

Or, perhaps it was not that it was not possible, but that it most definitely wasn't feasible the way we were going at it. We could get some gas into it, of course we could, but we couldn't manage to get enough in to make even a small balloon before a great hiss came back at us as the texture of the gum failed.

That was all it took, you see, one tiny part not to be as strong as the rest, and PAOH! Then we'd slump down upon ourselves and stay in our sizzly-sozzly condition until the effect of the N_2O wore off.

'We're going to have to try some other method.' Tom said what was so glaringly obvious I thought it didn't need said. So, I gave the obvious question as the obvious answer.

'Yes, but what?'

Therein lay the question. Therein lay our problem. Therein lay the quest of our manufacture if we were going to successfully negotiate this silly task we had set ourselves, and all before the cylinder of nitrous oxide emptied itself from our vain, but funny, attempts.

We needed to sit back and think carefully about what we were doing. We had to think of a strategy, a straightforward method that would somehow provide us with the means to fill liquorice bubble gum with laughing gas. And we knew we wouldn't find an answer to this problem in any of the scientific journals in the local library.

'Let's try one of Dad's pastry methods.'

'What?'

I didn't fully understand what I was talking about myself, so it was no great surprise when Tom questioned my opening remark.

'Okay, let's fill the biggest rubber balloon we can find with gas, right?' I needed a little bit of a pause here to help me think because I was kind of making it up as I went along.

Tom graciously nodded for me to continue.

'Then we can cover it with well chewed gum, stretched out to an even layer, like Dad does when he's covering something over with pastry.' Now that I heard it myself, it didn't sound like the worst idea I'd ever come up with.

Tom was thinking. I don't know if he was trying to think up something better, or if he was looking at me for the first time as the true genius I definitely might be. And then he spoke.

'That might work.'

'Of course it'll work.'

His words were confidence enough for me. I was feeling a lot surer of myself now big brother had given an idea of mine the nod of approval. And at last we had a theory, we had a plan, we had a way forward, and one that might yet rescue us from our predicament.

Over the following few days, we tried differing ways of mushing the liquorice bubble gum to its correct consistency for greatest expansion, but all to no avail.

The method that came closest to what we needed was a slow, soft heat in a pan of water. It was a bit too firmly fixed to itself because of the lack of pulping and so it couldn't expand the necessary distance to meet around the expanded balloon. There was only one thing for it – we had no option but to masticate the full quantity ourselves, although we did take advantage of a lot of it already being boiled to get us going.

Chew and spit, chew and sit, chew and spit, was what took up the whole of an entire Saturday afternoon. But at the end of our proceedings we had a big birthday balloon filled with N_2O, and we were carefully and neatly pleating large patches of liquorice bubble gum over its surface. Trying to keep it warm and moist until we had all the outer space of the balloon covered was the most difficult part of the enterprise, but we persevered until it was done.

With the hard work over, Tom and my eager self decided it didn't matter whether it was an outstanding success we were going to have or an outstanding failure;

either way, it should happen while we were out standing at a safe distance from the house.

So off we set to test our latest, greatest gassy idea!

Standing ready in the open air with our gummy creation, we suddenly felt extremely unready and very vulnerable within ourselves. But each not wanting to disappoint the other, we exchanged reassuring looks and rallied our determination to proceed, come what may.

As I held the wobbly balloon, Tom introduced a masterstroke of ingenuity and lightly tied a very long and very soft piece of string onto the bulbous bit at the end.

'This will give us the element of advantage when directing the balloon to where we want it to go.'

A little nod and a wink at the end of his explanation was more than enough to hatch a smile onto my face, too. It was a great idea and there was every chance of it working brilliantly.

I left it to Tom to try his hand at the balloon-flying business and one-handed manipulation of a single piece of cord. I didn't much fancy the idea of being the one whose tugs and pulls might get the blame for something going wrong. Anyway, it was his idea, his big idea, and he more than deserved first go at it.

Somewhat relieved, I stood and watched and waited as the nitrous oxide-filled balloon drifted slowly, heavily, ponderously, up toward the slim target of our aim. Up and up, in gradual increments of scale it made its ascent. Four eyes were glued to its rise, to the tautness of string feeding out from its great mass and down into the twist and leverage of what ran out from between Tom's right forefinger and thumb. Upward until it was nearly there, very nearly there, almost there.

And then it made it.

Our heartbeats were put on hold. We braced ourselves. We ducked our heads down as best we could while somehow still managing to look up.

We stood staring, waiting for something earth-shattering to happen, something wonderful, amazing, unbelievable, perhaps even magnificent.

Instead – nothing.

There was no explosion, no bang, no pop, not even a whimper of sound. And not a single word showed itself on the gummy balloon either. To say we were disappointed would be the understatement of the decade. We were utterly, bitterly, totally disappointed.

'There must be something in the nitrous oxide preventing it from showing.' Tom sounded even more disappointed than he looked, which was even more despondent than I felt.

This was his big idea and nothing had come of it. So we stood there, together in the disenchantment of real, happening and now. And while our eyes stared up at the gummy liquoriceness of balloon nestling contentedly against the telephone wire, our minds fell back into the challenge of jaw muscles and all the chewing and preparation that had gone into this momentous occasion.

We were completely stupefied. We stood there, magnificent in the mesmerism of all that wasn't happening for us.

What we now understood was that we didn't understand any of this. Just as we hadn't understood why it had worked in the first place, so we now didn't understand why it didn't work in the second place. And together, we couldn't manage a single word in consideration of what more than obviously was a non-event. So, we stood staring into the increasingly lost look of each other's withdrawing demeanour. Then we looked up.

We were just in time to catch sight of the saggy remains of a lot of masticated mis-effort give up the pretence of having something meaningful to do and flop sloppily back down to earth. A dirty splat rang through our ears when it met up with the challenge of hiding our disappointment on mother earth; and it failed miserably here, too.

We took turns to kick its ugly remains round the side of the house toward the bin. What was now booted out in front of us was a far cry, in terms of looks, from the magisterial innovation holding sway over the reckon of our thoughts up to but a few minutes before. Ah well, no doubt we'd be back at the drawing board soon enough.

It was only when we'd passed through the hallway and were halfway up the stairs that a lonely, lost thought gelled inside my head.

'Hold on. I think we may have missed a trick here.'

Tom hadn't a clue what I was on about; however, he had no choice but to pay attention to what I was saying because I blocked his movement upwards. Firstly, he looked at me, then he stared back into the emptiness of space I nodded toward behind, then he checked back into the immediacy of his own thoughts. However, nothing unusual registered upon, or in, his eyes.

'We've been stupid.'

I was still intent on getting him to see what I had just

seen, to try and catch what had only now popped into my head. The nod of my head and run of my eyes led his train of thought off through his look and back down the few stairs we had risen.

'What? There's nothing there!'

'Exactly!' My look left no doubt that I expected him to resolve this for himself, which he duly did.

'Siobhan's not there! She's not on the phone. But she's always on the phone. This means, she wasn't on the phone. There was no message because there was no signal!'

We looked at each other, into each other, each wondering at the other, as well as himself, for being so stupid, so obviously lacking in the basic charms of intelligence. Our two dull, slow-witted selves, retreated down the stairs and stood staring at the awesome presence of the telephone machine, this stupendous creation of near modern times.

I lifted the receiver and held it up to my ear. I listened. I could hear a voice calling me for the moronic plonker I so obviously was. Fortunately for me, the voice only sounded inside my head. But the buzz of the phone line did sound as if there was an extra element of humour running through it.

'We'll have another go at this tomorrow.'

'Provided there's someone using the phone when we do.'

Dozy Tom and my slow-witted self had a good laugh at ourselves as we headed off and made ready to right our woeful wrong-doing.

6 SHEER BALLOONERY

The next day, after masticating our way through countless packets of bubble gum, our new bubbly balloon, filled with N_2O, was ready. We only had one problem to solve – yet again the phone was not in use just when we needed it to be. And after all the chewing, I wasn't sure that I was still able to speak, but I knew I needed to try.

'Momsie, is it okay for me to use the phone now for a while?'

I don't know where my jaw got the strength from. I don't know how the workings within my mouth reconstituted themselves to form, package, and throw out, sound bites that even sounded like meaningful words to others. I was happy to have proven yet again to myself that the human body really is the most extraordinary of creations, since it was able to bring my mouth usage back from the brink of utter oblivion.

'No, he can't, Momsie. That's not fair! I've been helping you here all this time when I could have been, when I should have been, when I wanted to be, when I needed to be, talking to Wendy. And if I don't talk to her now, she'll be away at her dancing lesson and by the time she's back, I'll have my homeworks to do, and . . . and . . . it's just not fair!' Siobhan looked as if she was ready to swallow a great big huff of air, and even *I* didn't want this to happen.

'Oh, go on, then; see if I care!' I turned and left, as if in disgust at my sister always getting the better of me.

As I turned, I caught a look out of the corner of Momsie's eye. I knew what she was thinking. I knew she was really pleased at me. I knew she was well pleased to see I had developed, matured, because there was a time in the not-so-distant past when I would have fought the bit out with the whole world to get what I wanted. I couldn't help but feel well chuffed with myself; it wasn't too often I got a double whammy out of others.

Siobhan, on the other hand, was almost delirious with the joy of victory. I could see this not just in her eyes but in her whole demeanour as she swept past me in her hurry out to the hall. I so, so wanted to stick my foot out and trip her up. I so, so didn't want her to feel she was getting one over on me. But I knew I would have to bite my tongue, bury my pride, and the hatchet along with it, and say and do nothing. It wasn't easy but the thought of all that liquorice bubble gum going to waste meant this bitter pill was somewhat easier to swallow.

Straight outside I retreated, to the awaiting Tom who had been standing, bubbly balloon at the ready, and a length of string connected to one end which more than allowed for the reach of that one wire connecting us to the outside world.

Countdown was limited to a three, two, one, and off it was launched on its mission. Up, up, up, through the clearness of air above toward our target. And all the time, Tom guided and directed its course with little tugs and twists of the wrist, and small side-stepping movements of his controlling body.

Tom may have been in direct control but my absorption engaged me in every aspect of movement, every particular of direction. And the more I stared at the balloon, the more it seemed to me that it was controlling its master rather than the other way round. Strange, isn't it, what sillinesses can come upon you when you concentrate too hard.

Soon enough it was almost . . . almost . . . touching . . . and then it was there.

We could hardly believe our eyes. In the brightest, cleanest, sharpest picture imaginable, there appeared word after word after word of conversation, flowing first in one direction and then in the other direction.

Our eyes were glued to this spot, high above, where, like a television screen, the balloon brought to life words that were somehow, miraculously I suppose, finding their way down along miles of copper wire. Now, these same words were being beamed down to our two grinning mugs, as we smiled through the measure of each other and beyond our capability of understanding what was happening, from the stretched bubble gum screening high above.

We weren't interested in what our sis and her friend had to say. The words were irrelevant except insofar as they delivered the success of our do down to us. Our eyes were way beyond the immediate impact of knowing or caring about what Siobhan was cackling on about to Wendy, or vice versa; it was complete teenage girly nonsense. Our eyes were concentrated off in the completeness of knowing for sure and certain we had discovered something, something relevant, and perhaps even a major discovery of major importance.

I could see it all happening ahead of us, all the joy and congratulation, all the interest and attention; perhaps also, all the reward and adulation.

'It works! It works brilliantly!'

It was a rare occasion indeed that Tom ever managed to find himself excited about anything. Now was memorably one such occasion.

'We'll have to tell everyone. We'll tell Dad first. Then we'll show them all at school. Then Momsie can contact the newspapers and get them out to see, to witness, to photograph, to . . .'

In the middle of my wonderful flow of thought I was rudely interrupted by Tom.

'No, no, no. We'll not tell anyone. Not yet. This is only the start of our discovery. We shouldn't let anyone know about it – not before we've fully explored all possible outcomes. We don't know where or what this might lead us onto and we owe it to ourselves to try, try, and keep trying until we determine the fullness of our discovery.'

All the earlier chewing must have slackened the normally stringent muscle control Tom had over his tongue. I couldn't remember when last I had heard him talk so much, or with such fire in his breath. He obviously meant every word he said, plus a lot more left unuttered.

'Of course, not a word. Not a single, solitary soul will hear mention of it from me.'

I was with my brother on this one. We owed it to ourselves, as well as to the rest of the world, to see how far we could take our invention; to explore more fully into the realms of what we didn't know but were determined to find out about.

And when we looked up, even after all our mused mutterings, the stretchy balloon was still there, still parading word after word after word after word for the attention of our eyes, and the absorption of the grey spongy mass inside our well swollen heads. In the end, we had to give up on the balloon. There's only so much a body can take, and we had spent more than long enough in consideration of the inane musings of teenage female nonsense. We couldn't take any more.

A sharp tug on the length of string should have been enough to pop the gummy swelling of gas and release a blast of N_2O to the laughs of the world. Instead, the sphere of chewed gumminess remained intact as it floated down with every tug, tug, tug, and drawing in of the string.

'Great! We'll have this for future experimentation.'

I was thinking here mainly of my jaw muscles, my salivary juices, my stomach noises, plus all the blowing and puffing and expansion work we had to indulge in to make the bubble gum realise its full potential.

'And remember, not a word to Siobhan about anything she or her friend Wendy discussed.'

I was conscious here of the fact that while we had gotten away with it once, there was less than half a chance of getting away with it a second time.

I don't know whether Tom was listening to me. Every aspect of his stoical self seemed taken with ensuring no harm befell the well represented skin of balloonness entering the house in front of him.

Soon, the balloon was tethered to a bedpost, and one well away from the concerns of what being close to people and draughts and movement might bring. And as it turned out, this proved a great focus for our minds and a great draw for our concentrations.

I was increasingly of the opinion that we had determined the experiment beyond its own natural limits, for we hadn't expanded the concept of balloon-word development beyond its initial start. Tom was also uncertain of what path we should take with our discovery.

For days, then, the balloon caught the embarrassment of our looks every time we passed by our bedroom. Tom and my anxious self were each too honest to try and hide this truth from the other, and so we voiced our worries and concerns that we were unable to proceed. This helped, but only somewhat and purely in the very short term. Internally, I reckon we both were holding onto the notion that a eureka moment was going to strike one or other of us anytime now.

One aspect of our discovery did surprise us, though. After the first few days of our awareness being constantly consciously stricken by the visual aspect of the gummy balloon, we found it didn't do what we by now had expected it to do: it didn't deflate. No sagging with age took up residence on its appearance; in fact, quite the opposite took place. A definite tautness began to build up on the structure of the balloon as, somehow, it visibly began to grow in size.

'Did you add any nitrous oxide to the balloon?' Tom was carefully studying my reaction as he posed this question for me.

'Me? Why would I do something stupid like that?' I was amazed at him asking, and he knew by the frown of my regard, by the thrive of my words, I was as far away from doing something as silly as that as he was.

Our two scowls were then drawn over to the balloon, to study it more closely, but not too closely, in case it decided to have another little surprise in store for us, and explode in our faces. We mightn't have been the best looking fellas around but I kinda liked my facial features the way they were and I most certainly had no interest in reshaping who I was into who I wasn't.

We stared all around its outside, all along the stretched lines of its structure, and right into the void of gassy nothingness inside its lonely depth. But we didn't dare touch. We didn't dare breathe too closely on it either, in case the heat of our breath upset the fine balance of its existence.

It was a magnificent creation. We didn't say this; we didn't say anything of the sort because we didn't need to, this was staring right out of us. On the day we had filled it with nitrous oxide, the bubble gum appeared to be at full stretch. Since then it had grown and grown, expanding to almost twice its original size and, unless we were both mistaken, it was still growing.

'I wouldn't want to be lying on your bed when that explodes!'

My words were for Tom, but my thoughts were with myself because we shared the same bedroom and I didn't fancy the idea of being needlessly frightened out of my wits. Tom looked worried, but perhaps not quite as worried as *I* would have been had it been attached to *my* bedpost.

'We'd better shift it outside, then.' A definite hint of concern was evident in Tom's words.

'What are we going to do with it then?' A step in my direction followed through on Tom's words of worry.

'I don't really know yet, but let's decide when we get it out somewhere safe.' Tom muttered unconvincingly.

'I'll do it,' I bravely, foolishly, volunteered. 'You go ahead and open the doors, and make sure there's no one about. We wouldn't want this to explode in Momsie's face now, would we?'

Carefully, very carefully, extremely carefully, I eased the string off its hold on the bedpost. I didn't think it was possible to be so nervous and still remain upright and doing silly stuff at the same time.

I clutched firmly onto the string attached to the bulbous balloon and I tried to move as tenderly as I possibly could. I was absolutely shaking with fearfulness. After exiting the bedroom, every step I took down the stairs felt like my last.

Needless to say, Tom stayed well out of the way. He

held doors open all right, but all you could see of him was the end of a few fingertips, the rest of him was well and truly stashed behind the protective shield of each door. This was as close as he dared come to me, to the balloon, to the explosive charge so finely balanced within that would most surely impact upon me, upon us, upon the house, upon the whole world, with one wrong move.

So, for now, all I could do was take my time, watch every move of my body, every shake of my hand, while hoping and praying that the enormous build-up of latent energy I was transporting wouldn't explode all over me.

I stepped outside the house, trying to be even more careful than I had been inside, then—

BANG!!

7 SEEING IS BELIEVING

The magnificent thunderclap of a noise nearly caused my heart to fail.

Momentarily blinded, knocked senseless by the sudden impact of this noise upon my person, it was all I could do to remain standing, to hold onto myself, as I let go of the piece of string in my hand.

Amazingly, it didn't fall to the ground. Even more amazingly, it rose up through the air, there, in front of me, while I watched in awe and wonder and tried to continue breathing and get my heartbeat down to a sustainable level of thumpings inside my chest.

I was still standing, almost; I was still breathing, sort of; I was still conscious of what was going on around me – no, not quite. It was from the depths of wonder that I saw Tom appear before me, and he seemed to be smiling, and then it looked as if he might be laughing, and at the same time as all of this was happening, he appeared to be pointing and speaking. I had to concentrate extremely hard to gather in the facts as they represented themselves to me.

The balloon hadn't exploded in my face as I first feared. It was Tom. He had surreptitiously blown up a small rubber balloon and whilst holding open the final doorway, he had exploded it inside my ear. Or so it felt. I wasn't sure, I wasn't sure for certain, but it appeared as if Tom was laughing and pointing at me and he was saying something silly, something that really didn't make sense.

'Ha, I caught you! I got you back for earlier. That'll teach you to tell me it's going to explode over my bed!'

I could understand what he was saying, but as I began to gain more and more control over myself, his laughter became less and less funny to me. And in the meantime, my eyes followed off along the flight path of the liquorice bubble gum balloon filled with nitrous oxide.

Then Tom's eyes caught the follow of my eyes and together we watched as the big balloon snared itself on the edge of the roof high above. Instinctively, both our heads ducked down under the cover of our arms, as we expected our whole world to explode around us.

It's a fantastic feeling, being frightened, having the living daylights scared out of you by something of your own make, your own creation, your own incomprehension. That was it, you see: we didn't know the nature of the monster we had created. We didn't know the measure of its capabilities in any sense, either in a good way or a bad way. This meant we were totally at its mercy and positively at a loss as to what it might do to us.

We couldn't stay hidden under cover of our lack of protection for very long, especially when nothing as yet had happened, and most especially when it felt as though nothing was going to happen. So, we looked up. And when we looked up we could hardly believe what we were seeing because there, high above, snared against the corner of the house, the balloon sat, large as life. Now, however, no words were spread across the gummy surface. Now, stretched across its expanded exterior was a full colour picture, just like a television scene, and it showed men at work.

It took Tom and my curious self a few extended moments to catch our breath and capture fully inside our heads exactly what our eyes had tuned into.

What we saw was an everyday scene of men at work, working on a roof, a timbered roof they were now nailing down slates on, one by one. It was an old scene, it definitely wasn't modern. Two men were working, one on the roof, the other assisting him, carrying slates up the distance of a long, double ladder. There was no sound. There was no need for sound because the situation was self-explanatory, a perfectly simple and straightforward scene of two men hard at work in olden times. It was like a silent movie.

It was all very . . . leisurely. One man fetching up, the other nailing down. It was both fascinating and remarkable, and we knew what we were witnessing was truly unbelievable, yet it was there for our eyes to see. By now, Tom and my incredulous self were standing, shoulder to shoulder, unable to say a word, unwilling to speak or do anything that might break the spell, that might take away from us what we were now a part of.

Only those lucky enough to have witnessed at first

hand a truly remarkable experience, a beyond-the-ordinary proof such as this, can fully understand the state of limbo you're suspended in between the here and now you know you're part of, and the beyondness of time and belief in terms of how we're told life works and how we know we're meant to function.

There was no need for a reality check for the capture of our view. We were under no illusion as to the fact that what we were watching, what we were seeing, what we were absorbed into, was anything but real and true and happening, in a "had happened" sense.

The scene was ordinary, workmanlike in every sense of the word, and there was no asking in us as to the why we were seeing what we were being shown. It was there and it was occurring and this was more than enough for now, especially as it soon became obvious that it was *our* house they were working on the roof of. There was a freshness about it all, and the brickwork of the house seemed brighter. There was an emptiness of around, a few trees in the distance but a lack of growing and growth in the foreground, plus a lack of buildings all around. Just two men working away, earning their pay; two serious looking men who got on with their job and didn't stop.

Until now – when the one at the top of the ladder leant over to say something to the roofer, the one who was busily nailing slates down into their exact position, one by one by one by one. It was clear and obvious that what passed between the men weren't words of good humour; you didn't need to hear them to know they were words of strength and dark emotion. The look in the men's hard-working faces was what caught me most, what held the total of my regard. It was clear the men were in bad humour, that each was far from best pleased with some aspect of the other.

Then the words appeared to stop. It seemed to take them minutes but it probably didn't last for more than seconds as the action of two bodies met. Before the one trying to get off the ladder could establish his footing on the roof, the other man angled out with the sole of his thick boot and pushed him off the hold of the roof, off the tip of the ladder, and into the vast expanse of air through which he now fell. The shudder and thump of his weight ran up through me, up from the solid earth below, as I watched the body of this poor man hit the ground where we stood, and all trace of life was extinguished from him.

It took me a while before I could tear my eyes off this broken, misshapen wreck of humanity as I looked up into the blank, Godless features of the man above. Then he kicked the double ladder off its untethered hold before setting his snarled stare onto the lifeless figure beneath. My look followed the fall of his eyes down until I, too, caught the terrifyingly horrible sight of death lying motionless and still. Two trickles of blood ran out from his eyes; it was as if he was crying; crying the sorest, bloodiest tears ever.

My whole person was frozen in the hold of this stricken stare, for his eyes were wide open although he was very obviously dead. I knew the shudder that ran up through me iced through Tom as well. Both our looks were upon the gable wall of the house, our house, our home, and thence onto the face of the man high above, staring solidly, deadly, intensely down; and it felt like he was staring at us.

Then his neck straightened, stretching this way and that, as his head turned in every direction to see what was what, to see if anyone had witnessed what was what. Next, his mouth opened wide, and swallowed up all the noise that wasn't happening for our ears. It opened and opened and opened as wide as he could possibly manage as he called out, out into the distance of light and countryside around, for help, for someone to come and deal with the remains of this terrible deed.

I don't know if I managed to breathe even once during the whole time I was entranced by this murderous event. I know I must have but it felt as if my body was held in the same kind of suspended animation as what we were witnessing must have lain in for a long, long time, because all my concentration, and more, lots, lots more, was poured into the witness of this deadly sight.

Then a movement from Tom knocked me back a bit and had the effect of shaking the two of us from the stupor we were most surely steeped in. When we looked back up, we had just enough time to see a rush of other workmen come into the picture before it faded and disappeared, and left us staring up at the blank exterior of a balloonful of expanded liquorice gum. It was another few minutes before Tom and my astonished self were able to re-enter the domain of our true selves.

'What do you make of that?'

I neither knew what I was saying nor what I had to say, but I felt I had to say something.

'That was amazing. Unbelievable!'

Tom still had his sight stuck on the surface of the balloon. We stood and waited. We didn't know what we were waiting for. Perhaps it was for another sighting on the balloon, perhaps something else. We didn't know.

'We'd better try and get it down. See if we can save it for again.'

With the help of a step ladder and a stick – and an abundance of huffing and puffing and grunting and groaning – we managed to retrieve the balloon in one piece.

'We'd better be more careful in future,' Tom said as he grasped the trailing string tightly.

He didn't even bother to look my way when he spoke these words. For a mad moment I thought he must be taking leave of his senses, as he appeared to be entering into discussion with a balloon.

'What?' I needed to be sure of what was what if I was going to be sharing a bedroom with the mad scientist.

'I said we'd better take better care of the balloon. We could be onto something here.'

The broad nod that followed reassured me. Thank goodness for small mercies. It was one thing us all being a bit nutty on the inside, but to allow it to show on the outside, well, that just wouldn't do.

'What have you two got there?'

We weren't halfway up the stairs with our precious object when Momsie's controlling sound came from nowhere and nailed us each to the stair we were on. Embarrassment quickly seeped through our thoughts and onto the outer display of our skin.

'What? This? Oh, it's a balloon.'

'A big balloon.' For some reason I thought I should add my "big" word onto the end of Tom's stutteringly short description.

'I can see that.'

By now, Momsie's words were coming at us from the bottom of the stairs, but the look she added onto the end of her sound only served to add to the level of angst within. Silence ensued. A three-way serving of noiselessness changed the distance of a few stairs between into an expanse of miles, of years, of understanding.

'It's a scientific experiment we're engaged in, concerning contact and elasticity of product and associated connections of communication in its visual determination.' I loved it when Tom used his clever-speak to our advantage.

Tom smiled. I smiled. Momsie didn't smile. So, we all stood staring this way and that and the other, with two of us hoping that the third member of our triumvirate would show mercy and free us to do whatever it was we needed to do. We grew our smiles a bit, reminding Momsie these were her two darling sons who loved her dearly and, therefore, she didn't need to worry even slightly about what we would get up to.

'Just make sure not one bit of that messy stuff gets on the carpet in your room.' Momsie's voice softened and faded toward the end of her utterance.

'Aye, aye, Captain!!' As Tom and my happy self saluted, we broadened our smiles into great big loving embraces of looks, and Momsie very nearly smiled back.

'I'm warning you, the two of you, if one bit of that sticky stuff gets on anything – clothes, wallpaper, whatever – I'll have your guts for garters!' Momsie finished off her party piece and didn't hang around to hear what we had to say. We hurried up to our bedroom, hooked the balloon onto Tom's bedpost, and threw ourselves down to rest and regroup.

Throughout the following few days, we kept a close eye or four on the balloon, and to our tremendous sense of relief, it didn't appear to grow and it didn't appear to shrink. It seemed to have done all its expanding and contracting, and was now content to remain as it was.

When we eventually got round to talking about what we had seen, we reasoned the balloon had – magically, we supposed – tapped into a strong source of emotion that had lain dormant for as long as the house had existed.

Somehow, we understood that the balloon had made a connection with a part of the past in which a wrong, a terrible wrong, had been committed. And probably also a wrong that had never been righted, and so we were extremely curious about this.

So, after some deep discussion on the matter, we decided we'd better start dealing with the question absorbing so much of our attention.

8 SECRETS REVEALED

'Dad, how long ago do you think this house was built?'

Having agreed between us that the best way forward is always the direct route, I led off with my thoughts. Dad was well used to thinking on the hop; all parents probably are.

'Gosh, now there's a question out of the blue. Where do you get your ideas from?' Normally Dad would have been straight out with his answer; something told me he was stalling for time.

I let the question lie, entertaining my mouth with another forkful of food instead of picking up on the question served back to me. My eyebrows raised the question again.

Dad took his time with it; this time, he obviously wasn't too sure of the answer but I knew he'd know in general terms at least. 'I suppose it must be up fifty years or so. Wouldn't that be right?'

Dad sought Momsie's help here, but this wasn't going to win him any prizes because she had taken to studying the size or shape or something else of tremendous importance at the end of her fork. But he knew better than to put any pass on this and so he let it pass.

'Yeah, those are imperial bricks, bigger than the later metric ones. And the garage, it still has its original, metal framed window in it. It must be fifty years if not more. Why do you ask?'

There was no strength to anything Dad had said, except perhaps his last few words. All essence of vigour characteristic with knowing what you are talking about was absent from his voice.

'Was anyone killed while the house was being built?' Tom was definitely going to have to do something with his control of build-up, it just wasn't happening for him.

'Do you know, I believe there was. Wasn't he some relation of mine, darling?' Once again Dad aimed his answer at Momsie, seeking her help in something, but she didn't appear to want to hear much Dad had to say at the dinner table today.

A hush of silence flowed round those seated at table, in eyes that studied this way and that: this way to see what all the others were making of Momsie's vacant look; that way to see if there was any sign of Momsie snapping out of her reverie. It wasn't quite happening.

'From time to time Momsie gets a bad feeling about parts of the house, don't you, dear?' Dad appeared to have upped the ante on Momsie.

She looked up. She looked around all our faces, taking in the study of our determine – checking, calculating, evaluating, estimating, reckoning. We held our regard.

'Inside the house is fine. I would never live in a house

that didn't feel right. Outside, sometimes, in certain places, there's . . . there's definitely the sense of something wrong.' Momsie stared back down at her plate, but she seemed to have had her fill of what it had to offer. Then her mind took up the challenge of words for us.

'I tried to find out once. All I learned was that a great-uncle of your father's fell to his death some time during construction. There was mention of him working to a friend of his on the roof and . . . well . . . The rest was all gossip, malicious gossip.'

We all had stopped eating. We were waiting for more. More information concerning our house, and what we knew, the knowledge Tom and my anxious self possessed regarding it.

'Nothing was ever proven. But people talked. There was no love lost between the two men and, well, an accident like that, it leaves more questions unanswered than answered. It didn't matter much, though: the other guy went off to the war and became a hero, posthumously. And that, as they say, was the end of that.'

'We saw something. Didn't we, Liam?'

I nodded in agreement to what Tom had said, to encourage him to continue. He stalled momentarily, but then continued.

'We'll explain sometime later exactly how, but we saw a man being deliberately pushed off a ladder by his workmate. He fell at the far gable end of the house.' Tom pointed through his words.

Momsie nodded. 'I knew it. I knew it was there. I knew there was something there . . .'

'And now you can do something about it. Call Father what's-his-name tomorrow. He'll bless the outside and get rid of any demons thereabouts.' Dad tried to throw in a note of cheeriness through his interruption. Momsie nodded her agreement.

'What? And let a killer go free?' Siobhan had just shoved herself into an uppity position in her chair. She seemed determined not to want to let a killer go free.

'The man concerned died a couple of lifetimes ago. There's no point in pinning the guilt on his descendants, is there?' Dad looked around us. Tom and my eager self immediately shook our heads in agreement with him. Siobhan stalled but only for a split second, and then she fell in with the way of the rest of us.

'Well, that's enough of that sort of talk. Let's talk about pocket money. Who would like an increase?'

Unlike his words, Dad's smile bounced back off three flummoxed faces around him. His words burrowed slowly into the consciousness of deep within where they burned a lasting impression of all the extra enjoyments more power in the pocket would bring.

'I didn't think we had finalised anything here.' Momsie's eyebrows were raised in a questioning manner.

'Let's finalise them now, then.' This was Dad at his best, at his absolute best, as he normally was when it mattered, and as we wanted him to be at all times.

'Okay, guys, spill the beans.' Dad sounded semi-serious. He looked as if his face was ready to blossom into a smile or fall into a snarl. I knew what he was on about. Tom knew what he was on about. Together we were more than aware of what was coming our way.

All sorts of excuses popped into my head about how it didn't matter now, and how everything was all right, just let it lie, forget about it. I even thought about not telling the truth. Anything seemed preferable to the truth. Everything but the truth seemed to make the best sense. But I knew none of this would do, nothing but the truth would do now.

I looked over at Tom. As soon as our eyes met, his face fell away as he got stuck into some invisible scrapings on his dinner plate. I knew my brother. I knew him in one of these moods. I knew he could take a lifetime and a half to digest a single baked bean when occasion arose, as it seemed to have right now. We all knew this of Tom, and that's probably why Dad's look was concentrated on me.

The silence was becoming unbearable, and I knew that sooner or later it would fall to me to say what needed to be said, to sort out what needed sorting.

'Okay. Look, you see, you know the big balloon we made out of the liquorice bubble gum left over from . . . well, it's magic.' By now, even without any enthusiasm from three pairs of eyes seated around me, I could continue more fluently because Tom had packed in kicking at my legs under the table. 'Honest, it really is magic.'

I was looking for a bit of moral support from at least one of my listeners: a little crease around the lips, any sort of encouragement at all. I decided I needed to stall for a few moments to see what feedback came my way.

'Oh, how's that, then?' I would have expected Dad

of all people to be a bit more enthusiastic in how he delivered his words, even if he couldn't be in the actual words themselves.

A dry smile found the outer attention of my lips. 'Well, you see, when it comes in contact with parts of the past that aren't settled, it messages these through to us in the form of pictures of what happened. It obviously wanted us to do something, so the ghost of the past could settle, so the spirit could finally rest.'

There's nothing quite like getting the truth off your chest for making you feel good, especially when it's weighing too heavily on your mind. So, there, I had done it. I had said what needed to be said. And now it was all out in the open, the whole family's recognition of the truth would help Tom and my fretful self deal with it.

Out of the silence grew smiles, three smiles to be precise, and out of the three smiles grew three shaking heads.

'Right! Well, that's me finished. I'll wash tonight; who's drying?' Dad was up and away from the table before I had time to draw in a decent breath.

'I'll dry. You always were a great one for your stories.' Momsie tussled my tassled toss of hair as she rose to leave the table. She really liked what I had said. I could see this in her eyes, her face, her whole demeanour. Whether or not she believed a single word I said was a completely different matter.

'Yeah, Liam, you should take up fiction writing as a full-time hobby; you're very good at it!'

A dry, sarcastic smile hung on Tom's look. *Et tu,*

Thomas? I hadn't expected him to side with the others against me, against the truth. Then again, now I had had a couple of seconds to think about it, it became clear to me why he would.

Why should I be surprised at him not wanting me to make our secret known? I should have expected this. I should have seen it coming. But I hadn't and I didn't, and as things turned out, it was probably all for the best.

At least it had saved me from my normal torment of having to wash the dishes.

'What on earth were you playing at, telling them the truth?'

A short time later and Tom and my abject self were installed on the chairs in our room, with a neat pile of books in front of each of us, in a manner suggestive of our needing to do some schoolwork.

'What's wrong with telling the truth? *You've* even been known to do it from time to time!' I know truth is normally the final refuge for those devoid of the ability of telling a good lie, but, well, what was I supposed to do or say?

'What's wrong with telling the truth? I'll tell you what's wrong with telling the truth – they might have believed you! Think of the pickle we'd be in then!'

Tom was lifting, opening, closing and pushing away one book after another. His mind wasn't yet ready to get stuck into his studies. It was a no-win situation for me. So, if this was going to be the case, I reckoned it would do just as well both ways round.

'Who mentioned it in the first place? Who let the cat

out of the bag to Momsie? What sort of an eejit waves his magic wand about in front of people and then proceeds to state he hasn't got one? "A wand? A magic wand? Me? Oh no, I don't think so! Ask that other young man over there. Certainly not me!"'

By now my tone had become delightfully protesting, arms waving in the air, face taking up the challenge of showing deceit.

'What are you on about? And you can put your finger back in its socket before it falls off!' Tom then found what he had been looking for, something of deep, total and absorbing interest on the page in front of him.

I turned my head toward my own work. I had plenty to do, I knew I had plenty to do, but I was so entirely ill at ease within myself, so fretful, feeling so frustrated, I needed to do something, or say something at the very least.

'And another thing . . .'

I turned round through my words just as Tom did. I swiped clumsily round with an arm just as he did. Well, he may not have done so. He may have thought he needed to defend himself. Whatever the way of it, the two of us got stuck into one another, wrestling and thumping and pulling and hauling at any and every part of the other we could make contact with, and so we were off our chairs and all over the room.

We knew enough to know we needed to keep the noise down to a minimum, past experience having taught us this much. And so we grunted and growled, hissed and snarled at each other instead of howling and roaring and cursing and swearing, which was our want. Then disaster struck!

He said it was me. I said it was him. Whatever way it was, the end result was that the two of us were battering and battling it out around and on Tom's bed, and so we displaced something very dear to our hearts from its floating position off one of the bedposts.

KERPAWW!!

The mighty bang was all it took to bring us to our senses, but by then it was too late. In the flash that followed, Momsie was in the room, her eyes looking as though they were about to explode out of their sockets.

'What on earth is going on up here? Look at the state of this room! Well, neither of you is going to bed tonight until every last piece of chewing gum is off everything, including your two stupid selves. Now grow up, the two of you!'

No sooner, did it seem, had she appeared in the room than the door slammed behind her on her way out.

Thank goodness for the funny gas from the burst balloon. It had the immediate effect of shaking Tom and my bedevilled self out of the torment of torturing ourselves and each other, and took us up to the highest heavens of exist. Waves upon waves of hilarity rattled us for ages until we landed back on the shore of normality.

Only when the laughter was over and had done with us, were we in a position to attempt to fill our heads with schoolwork, and so we settled down to the do of it. This didn't last for very long.

'So, what do you reckon, then?' A very sober-sounding

Tom held his pen up from its page.

'I reckon we should bin as much of this gum before it decides to take up permanent residence wherever it has landed.'

Together we worked at it, picking strangely solid bits of gum up from here, there and everywhere, and dumping them into the waste-paper basket.

'No, I meant, what about the death, the murder? What do you think we should do?' A strong hold of hush ran through Tom's words, as if he didn't want anyone else to hear what we were saying.

'What can we do? There's nothing to do. It was too long ago. Momsie will do what needs to be done. We should let it drop.' I rose up onto my chair to continue my schoolwork.

'That's a cruel choice of phrase: "Let it drop!"'

The silence that followed from Tom, as he appeared to finish in mid-sentence, seemed laden with another focus, and I glanced over to see what was what.

It was the worst thing I could have done, for the two of us were off again, sniggering and giggling, joking and laughing, and having to wipe away tear after tear before we made a mess of the textbooks we were meant to be studying.

That's the brilliant thing about whatever part of our inner selves we were tapping into, the wonderful feeling in inner essence couldn't help but put on an outer show – until Dad entered the proceedings.

He had been sent. It was plain and obvious for us to see when he had been ordered up on a mission because it was there on his face, staring straight out at us. As usual, there was no doubting who had done the ordering – Momsie: we could distinguish this much from his features, too. What was plain and perhaps self-raisingly obvious, too, was that Dad was in his whites, with both hands covered in flour, so he wouldn't be amongst us for too long.

Our laughs dried up very quickly. Our smiles stayed and even brightened with the solid reflection of the same on Dad's jowl. You see, Dad was blessed with one of the most laconic of natures in the whole world.

'Sorry we were making so much noise, Dad, but we breathed in a bucketful of giddies from that N_2O stuff and we couldn't help ourselves.'

Here I had to hold in an explosion of laughter that wanted out of me. I tried coughing instead, coughing and coughing and turning my head away so he wouldn't see the watery flood of fun pouring out from my eyes.

'Do you need a hand with anything interesting? We've everything tidy here and we'd love to help with whatever you're working on at the moment.'

I don't know where Tom pulled this ability to be charming and sensible and helpful from. He looked and sounded the picture of the perfect son and had me won over straight away, and Dad, too, no doubt.

It did the trick. Dad's face brightened to a broad beam that shone first on Tom, then on me, as we stood smiling our happinesses back. The only problem here was, you never knew what you were letting yourself in for when you offered your services up to Dad, and we most definitely didn't have a clue what was to follow now.

'Good lads. That's what I like to hear. Come on down to the bakery as soon as you're finished your homeworks. I'll be ready for you then.' Dad imparted a nod of approval, probably more so for himself than for us, before turning and departing.

Having promised Dad a dollop of our time meant we'd have to get on with whatever needed getting on with in the intervening circles of the clock. So, homeworks were rushed and finished, and scant regard paid to the areas of study we should have paid more particular attention to.

And off we scampered into the unknowns of Dad's endeavours to make amends for our misbehavings.

9 STIRRING STUFF

'What took you so long? I was about to give up and go in and get Momsie and Siobhan to help.'

We were standing in the bakery, hands scrubbed clean in the beaming, smiling hope we were wanted for finer work than the normal stacking and cleansing.

Dad was no different to the two of us; he had patience for most things in life except for waiting, but he had obviously used his time to good advantage because everything seemed ready for us.

'Right. We're going to make marshmallows.' The unexciting sound ending his words made two young faces drop; it sounded really boring. 'Real marshmallows, look. I collected plenty of roots of that shrubby herb over in the salt marshes. It's all well prepared but, since we don't have a marshmallow beating machine, we'll have to do it all by hand ourselves.'

Dad was full of excitement, like a child with a new toy he'd been waiting on which was finally going to make his life complete.

Tom and my hesitant self donned our whites, rolled

up our sleeves, and readied ourselves to get stuck in. However, there was a little air of doubt hanging over us, and we couldn't mask its being there, not to ourselves. Eventually, I had to give in to the nag tugging away at the inside of my head.

'Is there much of a market out there for marshmallows? I mean, it's not the greatest of sellers and the market leaders do a pretty fine job in terms of product and price.'

I didn't like to question Dad. I certainly didn't mean to question him, and definitely not in terms of his own do. But I felt I had to say something in case he was leading himself up another blind alley.

'They do a good job, but we're not interested in that.' Dad didn't look up from what he was doing; he continued on with his preparation.

'So, why are we doing it if we can't compete with their product?' Thank goodness Tom had decided to enter the fray on my behalf, on our behalf, on all our behalf.

'Faith, boys, have a little faith.' After saying this, Dad obviously caught sight of two young men, no longer the two young boys he had known, and he realised he'd have to keep us properly informed to bring us along with him now.

'Okay. You know Mr German, the chemist?'

Two heads nodded.

'He and I have come up with a pectoral remedy, using a traditional method involving a decoction of marshmallow root. Those marshmallows you see in shops don't contain any marshmallow at all. Okay?'

Dad was smiling a hopeful smile that he was ready for action, ready to start, ready to get stuck in.

Two heads shook in response. We didn't know what to say and so we said nothing, absolutely nothing, which was the same thing as saying a lot, a whole lot.

'We make them. He sells them. We split the proceeds.' Dad's silly looking smile meant that was enough for us now, we weren't getting any more. And still we weren't happy. Not with what we were doing, where it was going, or anything else about the whole scheme. And, of course, yours truly had something to say about it.

'No one's going to want to eat the root of a marsh plant, no matter how much sugar you blend in to mask the taste. And they certainly aren't going to queue up in a pharmacy to get it.' There, I had said it. I had said what needed to be said, and in as nice a voice as possible.

'What are pectorals? What do they have to do with anything?' Tom added his bit of discouragement onto the end of, and probably to lighten the effect of, my tirade.

Dad put down his big stirring spoon, stepped away from the bowl, and came over to where Tom and my doubting self were standing at a loss within ourselves.

'You don't eat this product. It's for placing on your pectorals when you have a chest infection; that's why the chemist is involved.' Dad slapped his chest a couple of times in a monkey type fashion, as he tried to explain his thoughts to us. More than just a few seconds of silence followed as we deciphered exactly what he was saying.

'Ah, I see, it's a kind of alternative confectionery.' I

liked my little pun, which Dad managed to absorb into the serious side of his brain.

'Well, I suppose you could eat it. It probably wouldn't do you much harm. It might even do you some good. Yes, we'll have to look into that one.'

A dreamy state found its way onto Dad's look. We had seen him enter this internal mood of general abandon many times before and we thereby knew it was best to snap him out of it straight away.

'Show us what you want us to do.' Tom gave Dad a good strong nudge, nearly knocking him sideways out of his reverie.

'Right, the choice of agglutinant determines the texture of the finished product, which is always an important point to remember when selling to the general public. So, soak, sieve, mix, dissolve, stir, heat, stir, stir, stir. It's all in the stirring, men, so let's get on with it.'

Dad was well prepared for the small batch he had set out to make, and straight into it we went, stirring, stirring, stirring.

'This is stirring stuff!' Tom came out with the first joke of the session, and we had only been stirring for about half an hour. By this stage, I didn't think I still possessed the ability to command a funny look, not to mention think up a funny train of thought.

Meanwhile, Dad did all the important jobs: setting temperature, adding a little syrup to quicken, and a little warm water to thin, when he thought it was thickening too quickly.

'Jeepers. I'm going to have arms on me like Popeye

by the end of this.' I was gritting my teeth, pushing myself hard to continue on and on and on with the strainingly monotonous task of stirring, stirring, stirring. 'I'm already suffering from repetitive strain syndrome!'

'Yeah? I don't know about Popeye but you'll definitely end up with a girl like Olive Oil – Debra Rogers for instance!'

Because Dad's back was presently turned his way, Tom dipped a finger into the mix and flicked a shot of fluid over in my direction. However, it wasn't as liquidy as he had expected and he had to lick most of it off his hand before Dad caught onto what he was at.

'Struuuth!' Tom's face contorted into a poisoned picture of its former self. Brilliant! And hopefully my laughs helped add to his misery.

'Keep on with what you're at; another few minutes should do it.' Dad looked well pleased with himself, perhaps also with us. I think I would have been well chuffed with myself, too, if I had got two likely lads to do all the necessary hard graft while I pottered about setting, checking and overseeing what they were doing.

'What do you think, men; should we add flavour and colour? Remember, it's not to be eaten, it's to be worn as a sort of health patch on the chest.'

Dad was over now, standing between Tom and my knackered self, and his question and presence had the same affect on us both, our stirrings slowed down to a virtual standstill.

'Quicken! Quicken! Keep stirring, you're not finished yet.'

A couple of extra muscles in my right arm were fired into use by Dad's loud blast in our ears.

'If it looks better and smells better, what harm can it do? It can only have a positive effect on people, and make them appreciate its remedial qualities all the more.'

I was well pleased with Tom for having thought this through so logically and enunciated it so clearly. I don't know whether I could have said it any better myself.

'Is that a yes, then?' Dad peered over at the look of the two of us, and two heads nodded their positiveness back in his direction.

Anything to end this monotonous torture! I thought to myself.

So, Dad added the necessaries, and after another excruciating round of mixing, we were finally ready to blend together in trays pre-prepared to the required finished size. Thank goodness that was our involvement in the marshmallowing process at an end. It was not a minute too soon, for my right arm felt as if it had recently become detached from the rest of my body.

'Holy smoke! I think I'll be suffering from repetitive stirring disorder for the rest of my life. I'll be wakening up in the middle of the night, stirring my blankets. I'll be sitting at the dinner table, stirring my sausages and mash, and leaving my beans so they don't know where they are. I'll be in the swimming pool, causing a great whirlpool of a sensation by swimming round and round and round. And at school tomorrow I'll not be able to write, I'll only be able to spirograph; look!'

And with that, I walked round the big, centred, prep

table, and as I did so, my arm kept turning round and round and round as I went.

'Okay, men, that was brilliant. Thank you. I'll have these ready for Mr German by tomorrow morning. They should sell, what do you think?'

There was too much hope in Dad's judgment for my liking. And at times like this I became even more persuaded by Momsie's increasing insistence that Dad should take up a hobby such as gardening, or even fishing, or something equally as boring and mundane, instead of being trapped by these mad notions connected with confectionery.

'Perhaps we should pray for an outbreak of chest infections; nothing too serious, of course.' It only took a moment for Tom's smile to be reflected on Dad's countenance.

'Dad, do you not think maybe you should have made a few bigger marshmallow patches for some of your prospective female customers?' The twinkle in my eyes led off the naughty smile that had taken up temporary residence on my lips.

'Oh no, they can buy two each! Away you go, lads, and thanks again.'

Dad turned away from us and back to the service of his work. But we could tell he was smiling, for we knew he enjoyed the odd bit of banter with us about things like that.

And off to the land of Nod we departed, totally stirred out.

10 MERLIN'S MAGIC

Next morning and we were with Dad when he delivered his wonderful cure for wheezy, coughy, coldy, chest infections to the pharmacy. We carried in four each, all carefully wrapped in greaseproof paper, with a very simple but effective Red Cross painted on top. Momsie had also made an advertising board to stand atop the wonderful creations of Dad's make and bake.

Merlin's Magical Chest Enhancers was what Momsie had chosen to call them, and nobody at home was brave enough to disagree with her. What would *we* know? What would *any* of us know? Momsie had a talent, a flair, for this sort of thing and far be it from Tom or my fearful self to raise a question mark over what we were vehemently assured was the correct title.

After finishing off the normal run of deliveries with Dad, it was off to school with us; off and into the normal patter of routine that sat so well with us; and that was us for the day.

By evening time, we were all seated around the dinner table when, all of a sudden, the phone rang. Disappointment stretched across Siobhan's demeanour after she had jumped up from her seat to answer. It was Mr German, the pharmacist, and he wanted to speak to Dad.

'Good . . . good . . . good . . . good . . . that's great . . . good . . . good. Double the number for tomorrow, then, that's absolutely no problem. Thank you. Goodbye.'

Down went the receiver and up went our eyes to catch the smiling happiness of Dad's bright face; while a couple of trapped muscles cramped and complained inside my right arm and shoulder.

'We're onto a real winner here. The whole lot we left in this morning sold out within hours. Isn't that brilliant?'

Every muscle in my body flexed at the thought of double the amount of stirring tonight. Ah well, whatever was needed was needed, and if it had to be done we'd do it, much and all as we might not like it. Tom and my resolute self wouldn't shirk our responsibility, even if it meant staying up beyond midnight.

It did.

We were stirring right-handed, left-handed, clockwise, anti-clockwise, single-handed, double-handed, continually stirring, stirring, stirring. Even when it felt as if our arms had completely unwound themselves in their sockets, we had to keep going because to stop would have run the risk of not being physically able to start again, not to mention the chance there was of ruining the mix and having to start afresh. So, we kept on going and going, stirring and stirring, because we had to, even though it felt as if our arms had completely detached themselves from what remained of our living, breathing selves.

Therefore, completely done out, we said our good-nights to Dad who had to work on into the early hours of the morn, before beginning his normal early routine with the bakery business. We felt sorry for Dad, there was no doubt about that. We felt a lot sorrier for ourselves, there was definitely no doubt about that.

Together, side by side, Tom and my exhausted self stood at the sink in the bathroom, staring pityingly upon the reflections of the two weary sods in the mirror. We tried to laugh. We couldn't. The reason why we tried to laugh was because it was as much as we could do to hold a toothbrush in hand.

'I can't do it. I can't clean my teeth. My right arm doesn't know it's still alive and my left arm's gone on strike, permanently.' Tom was the same as me, except he could talk; neither of us having managed to squirt even a tiny splodge of toothpaste onto our brushes.

The steady trickle of the cold-water tap held the fall of my look. My eyes seemed to have control over the rest of my person, and they were determined to do one thing – close. I just wanted to fall into bed and sleep, sleep, sleep, even until the morning, when I knew I wouldn't want to get up for school. But, in between times, I could enter the sheer bliss of the voluptuousness of hours spent with eyes closed and head steeped in the luxury of my pillow, and sleep easing through the reckon of my fatigued body.

'I'm too tired to bother. I'm away to bed.'

I don't know where I dug up the strength to speak from. I let my toothbrush fall into the catch of the sink.

I didn't care if it was morning or night-time, I was going to my bed. I crossed the landing, and by the time I entered the bedroom, I had just enough energy in reserve to drag off my outer garments, fall upon the open invitation of my bed and thence into a deep, deep sleep.

'Tom, Liam, get up . . . NOW!'

It might have been minutes later, it could even have been days later, perhaps even weeks, but when eventually I did manage to respond firstly mentally, and then physically, to Momsie's blastings of the air, it was a great bonus already being half dressed. All I had to do was splash some water in the general vicinity of my face, drag on my school uniform, and – hey presto! – I was ready for school.

Strange looks fell upon me from Momsie and sis as soon as I made my appearance in the kitchen, but only Momsie transferred her thoughts into words.

'You're looking particularly, how should I put it, yes, dishevelled this morning. If I didn't know you any better I'd say you slept in your school uniform last night.'

There was more of a look of wonder than reproach in the glued stare of her eyes. I couldn't think what was wrong with the way I looked but my mind was elsewhere.

'Thanks, Momsie, you don't look so bad yourself!'

A very tired smile followed on through from the words of my jest. My eyes felt as if I must have swallowed a packet of tablets that make you squint, that irrefutably made my regard askew and aslant, as I was only just able to see through them. Externally, I wasn't about to agree with Momsie. Internally, however, I couldn't disagree with her. I felt a bit, well, grubby, manky, unkempt, but I didn't mind this at all.

It wasn't long before we were out the door and off to school, eventually, and I must say that as the day wore on, this feeling of grubbiness I had been made aware of only increased in multiple factors. I knew then I should have changed my nags at least, my socks as well, and I fully determined this business of sleeping in your clothes and trying to function as normal the following day wasn't for me. To prove this point to myself, as soon as I got home I washed away my iniquities and cleansed my skin of the tackiness of its feel, even though the water in the system wasn't much above lukewarm.

Tom and my cleansed self were almost afraid to look at Dad, and we were definitely afraid to ask why he had a cast-iron grin moulded onto his face, when we all sat down to dinner later on. Our feeling of dread didn't have to wait very long to find out what was what.

'Guess what?' Dad had hardly managed to swallow the first bite off his dinner plate before he started his guessing games.

Neither Tom nor my empty self could bare the thought of encouraging him straight away. At least let us get a few morsels of food into our systems before announcing more orders from Mr German, the pharmacist – and more frightful exertions for our bodies.

'Yes, Dad, what is it?' I don't know where Siobhan stole her pleasure from. She never normally suffered from initiatory moments such as this.

For my own part, my food had suddenly lost its *joie de vivre*. More than that, my mouth had lost its desire to chew, as well as speak, as my mind had lost the will to absorb what was surely coming next, as my ears had most definitely lost all determination to fulfil their primary function.

'What is it, Daddy? Something good, yes?'

Siobhan had reverted to type, to how we knew all girls really were, no matter what age they were, how ugly they may have appeared, or what prettiness may not have suggested.

Dad was stalling with his answer, looking over, waiting for Tom's and my avoidance regard to turn his way, waiting for us to join him in his feeling of good humour. I was about to say . . . no, I wasn't . . . but I *wanted* to say that if this was another double order then he could forget about it, because he could forget about me, he could forget about Tom and me because we were worn out! Fortunately for me, Dad spoke first.

'I had another phone-call today from Mr German. And guess what?' Dad's excitement spread quickly through to Siobhan and Momsie.

I was about to spit, to spit fire, and Tom looked as if he had already choked on something unpalatable.

'What, darling? Tell us, quickly!'

Momsie's words, backed up by her and Siobhan's unintelligent look, confirmed in my mind that the two of them were going to do the stirring tonight, because it definitely wouldn't be Tom and my disgruntled self. Anyway, we had far too much homework to do and it was likely we wouldn't be finished before midnight.

'His suppliers want me to supply them, so they can put Merlin's Magical Chest Enhancers into every chemist shop in the area; and if this takes off, we'll be going nationwide!'

The look on Dad's face indicated he had no intention of eating his dinner tonight. In fact, he looked so perfectly pleased with himself, he'd probably never need to eat another dinner again in his life! Likely, too, Tom and my disconcerted self would never be able to eat dinner again either, because, after tonight, we'd probably lose the ability to operate with a knife and fork, so muscle-bound would we be from all the stirring activity ahead of us.

Whatever it was that had taken control of the inside of my head seemed about to explode. I could hardly cope with the volume of *oh nos* building up inside, wanting out, needing out, demanding to make themselves known. The look coming across from Tom was exactly the same, except he was waiting for me to air my views for the two of us.

'Dad . . .' I had started to let it all out; I had got it all together inside my head – what to say, how best to say – when Dad interrupted me.

'Don't worry, son. My two men can put their minds at rest, and your arms back in your sockets, because today I invested in a present for us all – a state-of-the-art, marshmallow-beating machine. And it's here all the way from the United States of America. Well, what do you think of that?'

Dad looked triumphant. He looked magnificent. He looked like he was king of the whole world, as he was of our world. I wanted to hug him and thank him from the depths of all the sinews of all the muscles in my right arm, both my arms, in fact. But Momsie was there first, and it looked as though she had no intention of ever releasing Dad from the stranglehold of the hug she held him in.

A moment or two later and none of this really mattered to me because a sense of feeling had returned to my body, and with it, a sense of taste to my mouth. Now, I was hungry, really hungry, and I began my devour of every last scrap of food on my plate.

'This is the big one, darling. I know for sure and certain now, we're going to make it big with our magical marshmallow invention. If they're selling so well now, just think how many we're going to need for wintertime when chest problems really take hold!'

Neither Momsie nor Dad had any intention of ever finishing their dinners. They were in a world of their own now, together. A world of freedom and enjoy, and real recompense for all the long, hard years of sweat, toil and endeavour they had both put in. By now, too, Siobhan was over hugging into the two of them, while Tom and my blissful self indulged our minds in the future sunshine of so much return for so little effort.

'The machine's not new but it comes fully guaranteed. Guaranteed to make us our first fortune! This will mean I'll be able to follow up on all those ideas I've had and, with the right investment in them, we should see another couple of winners!' As Dad's smile shone out its blinding brilliance, Momsie's shrunk to a fraction of the size it had been.

'One thing at a time, dear. There's no point in giving yourself a whole lot of bother when you don't need to.' By now, Momsie only had the remains of a fragile-looking smile clinging onto a worrying frown.

'Of course not, darling . . .' Dad was always a good one for falling in with whatever it was Momsie would propose. 'But I might as well, anyway.' Except for this time, it seemed.

A mixture of different silences held sway over the remainder of our eating proceedings. What was normally such a loquacious event, and should have been even more so today, had become uncommonly hushed for most of us. Dad, meanwhile, was away off with a whole bounty of thoughts concerning what experiment he was going to conduct next and next and next. Poor Momsie – she had only managed to settle her feet in the comfortable feel of this new ground called success, when Dad had scuppered her dreams and lifted her mind up through the dreamy blankness of his fantasies.

By now, too, Siobhan was tripping over herself with the wonder of what shop she should visit first, and what she should buy, and what colour would suit her best, and what all her friends would have to say, and so on, and so forth, and fifth, and sixth. While Tom and my relieved self were settling our minds into the gladness of our bodies with not having to go stir crazy with any more work like the previous night's.

I must admit to having my thoughts stolen away from me for a time, and Tom was no different, as we, too, fell into the wonder of Merlin's Magical Chest Enhancers. Tom and my earnest self went out on more and more delivery runs with Dad, but this, too, didn't last, when it was decided a van and a man would come and collect from him.

It wasn't long before we missed this getting-outness, and I guess Dad did, too, because meeting and greeting and being in the company of others was a real part of his comfort. He loved the jokiness and banter and socialising process that accompanied quick deliveries into chemist shops. If I missed the nods and winks and nuances and nudges when I was only the occasional helper, how much more must Dad have missed all the laughter and gestures and carry-on associated with our product?

'I haven't a clue what the shop girls are going on about half the time; I think the generation gap is beginning to tell.' And Dad would laugh to himself for our benefit, and we would join him in a little light loudness of relief, for his benefit.

Then something wonderful happened that turned to dust.

11 HAPPY SNAPPY

There had been a few phone calls and lengthy conversations with various members of the media, and so, after a few brief interviews with the local newspapers, a date and time was set for the big event – one of the national tabloid dailies was to arrive and do a major piece. Such a fuss it was, too. Everything was arranged with plenty of product set out for the photo-shoot which was the most important part of the event.

Siobhan spent weeks preparing herself plus an ever-broadening circle of friends for this joyous, this momentous, moment in our family's history, when her good looks would be captured for a whole nation to see.

Momsie only spent days arranging every aspect of her self, from hair style to what she was wearing would look like, depending on whether she was standing or sitting. In the end, she decided a very feminine look was what was needed, and there was nobody brave or foolish enough in our house going to say no to that.

Dad took hours to sort out the finer details of himself, with facial hair being his speciality subject; lack of it in one crowning quarter being more than counterbalanced by the copiousness of such in areas of nozzle and lugs.

Tom and my cavalier self didn't give this matter of appearance any quarter. On the morning in question, we thought we were sorted, turning up as we were, only for Momsie to chase us back upstairs to do specific readjustments with areas of self we never would have bothered about. When we arrived back down, after deliberately taking our time with water and soap and comb and collar, the newspaper guy was already in with the photographer.

Momsie had kindly supplied them with a few bowls of her special chocolate porridge to warm them up and get on their inside good sides. After several slurpy scoops and much appreciative asking for seconds and thirds – and even some cheeky requests for takeaways for their own young snappers, which Momsie smilingly supplied – they soon were snapping and yapping away. In fact, as we re-entered the room, Siobhan had been asked to stand aside, alongside Dad, and the photographer poured all his energies into Momsie.

'Stand over like this. Bend forward. Stretch your head back. Push your arms out to the side. Shoulders back. That's it. A bit more out to the front. Push it out a bit more. Bend forward. Right down. That's it. Right down, so I can get it all in. That's it! That's what we want! Good girl! That's more like it now. And again. That's it. All the way down. And all the way out. Perfect!'

The photographer talked through his camera, not removing it once from the focus of his eye while he spoke.

Momsie was thoroughly enjoying the concentrated focus of all his attention. Siobhan's face was descending into a snarl of anger and exasperation. Dad seemed oblivious to all that was going on around him, so busy was he chatting to the man over by the door who had pencil and notebook in hand. This reporter looked as if he had recently been snared in a big way by a bigger mousetrap that had left the biggest slap of an indentation in the middle of his face. Add to this the fact that he looked as if he cleaned his teeth in Brasso twice a day, every day, and you will get the picture of what we were dealing with. It was a very unsavoury sight indeed.

The photographer waved Tom and my uneasy self away from Momsie, who was bent over, hands upon her knees, being snapped from a very cute front angle. And so we stood, trying to smile as pleasantly as we possibly could, keeping one eye on the proceedings over with Momsie, one eye on Dad's answerings to the rodent-face he was with, and one eye wondering where on God's lonely earth our sane and sensible parents had gotten to.

I don't know what was going on in Dad's mind, answering any and all stupid questions thrown his way.

'So, Mr Baker, when did this idea first pop into your head?'

'I *am* a baker, a master-baker, it's not my name . . .'

Here the reporter's nods encouraged Dad to hurry up.

'And I first came up with the idea when—'

'Would you say you had any other talents with regards the female form?' The question was asked very directly, a bit too directly. I could see Dad was stumbling inside his head but he answered as best he could.

'Oh, you'd have to ask my wife that one. I'm a baker, and I spend my spare time trying out—'

'So, Merlin's Magical Chest Enhancers was your idea?'

'Yes, I'd been working on a number of different recipes . . .'

'And who did you first try it out on? Your wife?'

'Well, actually, yes. Caroline wasn't feeling the best and I thought it would be a good idea—'

'I think we can all see what a good idea it was. Now, that doesn't leave much to the imagination, does it?'

At this point, the photographer leered over at Momsie and I saw what he was going on about, but I immediately chastised myself for thinking so poorly of someone, for thinking that a grown man would behave in that way. Dad was lost somewhere in the space between where he stood staring wonderingly over at Tom and my befuddled self, and the nods he sent off in the direction of this space cadet of a reporter.

'So, Mr Baker—'

'Mr White!'

'What?'

'I said I *am* a baker.'

'Yeah, that's what I said.'

'No, you called me *Mr* Baker.'

'Aren't you?'

'Yes, I *am* a baker, but—'

'Ah, I see. You'd rather be called something else for this. I understand. No problem. Absolutely no problem at all.' The cretin of a reporter had changed his look from nodding to tapping his nose with his forefinger and winking one weaselly eye at the same time.

'Are you stupid?' Dad's tone caused all eyes belonging to his family to stare over at him. Rarely, if ever, did we hear him raise his voice, not to mention fire an arrow as blatantly as this.

'Well, I wasn't top of my class at school, if that's what you're asking.'

The reporter reckoned the disarming grin he now sported should work for him. I suppose, the more we looked at him and listened to him, the more we undoubtedly felt sorry for him. Dad relented and softened his tone.

'My name is Mr White. My profession is a baker. I came up with Merlin's Magical Chest Enhancers more by accident than design and they're—'

'Selling like hot cakes all over the country. Making plenty of money, eh? Making lots and lots of the lovely dosh, eh? Making plenty of women happy, and men, too, for that matter, eh? What's your success rate?'

'My success rate? I don't know, I haven't yet—'

'You haven't had any failures? Brilliant! And is it true that one of the country's leading bra manufacturers is in negotiation with your firm to include your product as padding in one of their more upmarket ranges?'

'I suppose that's not a bad idea . . .'

'So, you don't deny negotiations are at an advanced stage? Excellent! When are you going international? When do you expect Merlin's Magical Chest Enhancers to burst onto the world stage?'

'Well, I couldn't honestly say . . .'

'Quite right; keep them guessing. Build up the expectation and with it the price. Excellent marketing strategy!'

'Thank you.'

'No, we must thank you. Merlin's Magical Chest Enhancers have already worked their wonders on many hundreds of our fair sex. Tell me, the tingling sensation reported by some users is normally followed by a very engaging side effect; did you plan it this way?'

The reporter's pencil was scribbling away, even before he heard a word of an answer.

'With every medical cure there will always be a side effect, but there's no possibility of it being anything serious or long lasting with our product.' At last, Dad managed to finish a sentence.

'The very opposite of unpleasant, I'd say; the most pleasant of side effects for all concerned. Nudge, nudge; wink, wink; say no more, say no more. Know what I mean?'

As the reporter seemed to lose the plot completely, indulging in juvenile behaviour that was lost on Tom and my bewildered self, Dad turned round to the support of our eyes, as we all shrugged off these strange actions of the stranger in our midst.

'Right, it's a wrap!'

A loud smack of his hands followed on from shoving dog-eared pages into his jacket pocket, and straight toward the door he headed, with his poor photographer colleague trying to grab and go in his wake.

'Monday's edition. People like a good lift at the start

of the week. You don't have to ask what page it's on. We'll be in touch. See ya!'

With that, the sleazy reporter and his sidekick, the confused cameraman, were out the door and gone. And a deep feeling of relief eased into all present in the house again.

'What in God's holy name was that all about?' Dad stood there, bewildered and confused.

'Don't ask!!' Tom and my suspicious self landed out the same answer at the same time.

'The photographer seemed very nice; very good at his job.'

We all stared over at Momsie, with the same wonder probably foremost in all our heads: *could she really be so innocent? Or so naïve?* In my own mind, I opted mostly for the former, with just a hint of the latter added in for good measure.

'He wasn't interested in me! Why wasn't he interested in me?' Siobhan was very far away from looking best pleased with what had taken place.

'Lean forward in front of a mirror some time and you'll not see for yourself!'

Tom gave me a nudge as he shared a bit too much of his inner thinking with the rest of the family. We were on the same wavelength, but something inside my head reckoned it best to keep schtum on this one.

'Now, now; that's enough of that. Your sister's still young; she's got plenty of growing still to do.' Momsie straightened herself up and fixed herself at the front.

'What?'

'What?'

Dad first, Siobhan next, let out an indignant exclamation while staring crossly at Momsie.

'Don't come on the innocent with me. You know I didn't fill out fully until after the children came along.' A very pointed smile headed Dad's way. He caught it but he didn't know what to do with it. Momsie then turned her attention toward Siobhan.

'Your turn will come, darling, don't worry about it. You know the sort of newspaper it is, they're always on the lookout for glamour, that's all they want.' Momsie's smile was so big on the inside, we couldn't help but catch a lot of it on the outside.

'That's one way of describing it!'

I knew I shouldn't have, but I couldn't help myself, I couldn't hold in what was at the forefront of my mind, wanting to be heard. And thank goodness I didn't let any of the rest of my thinking escape.

As it was, as things stood, as it panned out, all eyes had me in their hold, were fixed on my person. Silence ensued. I didn't know what was going on in all the rest of the heads present, but I had a fair idea. Unfortunately for me, they all seemed to have more than just a fair idea of what was buzzing around inside my head, and they seemed intent on waiting for it to come out.

'Go on, then, share with us what is on your mind.'

Dad was insistent. I knew his tone. I knew there would be no let-up from him until I spilled out exactly what was on my mind. I tried stalling for a few moments, but there seemed little point; there was only one way out of this for me.

'Are you lot blind? Could you not see what was going on there?' As I began, Tom raised his eyebrows in an *oh dear* kind of way. But I wasn't going to stop now.

'They've got the wrong end of the stick . . .'

'Don't be silly, they're from a national daily.' Dad's interruption was as pointless as it was ineffectual. So I continued.

'It's not that they don't think Merlin's Magical Chest Enhancers isn't what it is, it's that they think it is what it isn't.'

I hadn't a clue how I was going, not to mention how I was going to say what I had to say. Three sets of eyes stared at me in the disbelief of what I was saying; the fourth, Tom, saved his disbelief for the fact that I was saying what I was saying. And he looked as if he was enjoying the excruciating standpoint I had plonkered into. But I had to continue.

'They think Dad's invention is designed to enhance the size of the chest, in women, if you know what I mean.' I didn't want to say anymore. I wanted to let the penny drop, or at very least, to see if the penny *would* drop.

Moments later, and Tom added to my measure as well as to the incredulity stamped on the faces of the other three, for he held his shirt out at the front, in two very specific areas of frontal posture, while nodding his head and holding in an enormous burst of laughter.

Momsie's face turned bright beetroot purple – it didn't even go red first. Dad's face held all the inner fears of a stricken conscience. Siobhan's facial muscles were alternating between preparing to laugh and preparing to cry. My regard bounced from one to another to another and then round to Tom, who by now had his two arms angled up and his hands opened out in a questioning manner. There was the distinct influence of dumbfoundedness among us, as a lot of different small things began to come together inside heads and make a complete and different sense of what had gone before.

'Oh holy God almighty, he wasn't trying to catch my face at the right angle – he was trying to catch the cleft of my cleavage!' Momsie's horror-struck face stared across at Dad, as she automatically caught hold of the bulk of herself out front.

Dad couldn't say anything: his look was beyond embarrassed dismay, his thoughts were running too deep and too fast for him to catch hold of one and air it to the rest of us. Siobhan looked crestfallen; her eyes were cast down over her frontal aspect.

'So that's why he didn't want to take my photo, the dirty, rotten, low-life!' A sudden glint became apparent in her look, as her mind was off and travelling along a different vein of thought. But, unfortunately for sis, she aired her new thoughts, too.

'Maybe there's some truth in it! Maybe it really does work!' Excitement had so obviously taken hold of her, she was finding it difficult to contain herself where she was. 'I have to make a phone-call!' And with that, she was off – almost.

Momsie stepped across her path and blocked any chance Siobhan had of escape. 'No one's going anywhere until we resolve this!' While she spoke, Momsie looked across at Dad, in pursuance of his thoughts and feelings on the matter. It took a few more moments before he spoke.

'I can't believe it. Is that why they've been selling so well, because people think – because women think – they increase the size of them, there?' Dad nodded specifically toward Momsie's frontal aspect.

A lot of heads were now nodding around him.

'My goodness, this is truly amazing, unbelievable. And we'd better cash in on it before the truth comes out!'

The look of disbelief on Dad's face was as nothing in comparison to the incredulity smacked across the four faces surrounding him. We could hardly believe our ears. This most definitely wasn't the moral tone we had expected to hear from him. This seemed very far removed from the solid moral judgment we could always rely on from Dad. And it certainly cast doubt in my mind.

Maybe he was right. Maybe we *should* cash in on a lucky break now that we had the chance, because, as Momsie was always saying, we needed the money. Okay, we all knew what she meant. We didn't actually *need* the money, but it would go down very well providing this and that and the other for the house, plus all the extras we could be doing with for ourselves but always had to do without. Dad might just have a valid point here. In fact, he could very well have knocked the nail on the head as far as all our creature comforts were concerned.

'Good idea, Dad. This could be the winner we've all been waiting for!' I couldn't help myself, letting my thoughts explode out like that. And I was immediately backed up by Tom, who added a vociferous 'Yeah' to my words.

We looked at each other. But now with eyes that could see the other dressed in the latest fashion, all the new style, instead of our normals of what would wear best and didn't cost a fortune. We could suddenly see ourselves with fantastic watches, all the latest gadgetry, plus all the paraphernalia of modern existence that so far hadn't touched our lives. In fact, we were walking, living, breathing advertisements to the fact that in life and living, you didn't need any of it; but now it was possibly possible, we so, so wanted to have all of it in our possession.

Now, we could see all the extras coming our way for all the years ahead, all those articles of adornment and attire that would make us all the more conspicuous, respectable perhaps, desirable definitely. All the trappings of success we so wanted to have as our own, to make part of us, so we, too, could be the bright young things so obvious when they were around.

'You can cut that nonsense out for a start!'

Momsie looked over at me as she threw out her feelings a bit too forcefully. Thankfully, her stare didn't settle too long on my regard but hopped onto Tom and thence onto Dad. It was there, on Dad, that her eyes took root and settled themselves for a long, hard stare.

'We'll not profit from the insecurities of others, of those less fortunate or more fortunate depending on your view. I'm disappointed at any of mine wanting to make financial gain from a falsehood. It's a shocking thought, and it's wrong, so very, very wrong.'

As she chastened our minds with her words, Momsie instinctively buttoned up her blouse more than she would normally have done. I felt like bringing this to her attention, especially in relation to how unbuttoned her blouse was when the national daily's photographer was snapping at her frontal chasm. I said nothing.

'But how is it wrong if we continue doing what we've been doing? For all we know, it might work as a breast enhancer as well as a chest enhancer!'

Dad tried his smile on round the rest of us. It suited very well. We smiled back. He didn't bother to try it on with Momsie. Instead, he raised his eyebrows more in hope than expectation. Unfortunately, Momsie's demeanour indicated she wasn't for yielding an inch. Her lips were cemented together so none of her sour taste, so evident in her look, could escape.

'Okay, then, what do you suggest we do?' A wily smile took hold of Dad's countenance.

Momsie had to think about this one. It was obviously easy enough to state what *shouldn't* be done, but now she was having difficulty coming up with even one suggestion as to what *should* be done. We all held the look of Momsie's blank expression; her absence of words were foremost in our hearing. And so it took a while before Momsie could change the angle of her mind into words.

'I think it might be best to do nothing, and say nothing, until we see what happens after next Monday. I don't know how I'm going to face the world if they print the wrong angle of me alongside a piece carrying the wrong angle on Merlin's Magical Chest Enhancers.' Momsie wandered off, leaving our minds to the consideration of what she had said.

Ever-practical Dad, however, wasted no time in worrying and used the next few days maximising his production. It was full steam ahead for Dad, along with any and every bit of assistance Tom and my ardent self could offer.

And so it was left that all we could do was wait and see what angles would materialise, as well as what response would materialise, in Monday's paper.

One consolation for us youngers was that our mid-term break was also due next week so we had time to cope with whatever fallout befell us.

12 GRANDA P: THE 70-YEAR-OLD BOY!

There are some things in life over which you have no control. One of these events just happens to be when your parents suddenly decide to dislocate you off by train to the countryside, and your much-loved but undeniably eccentric Granda P, for the complete duration of a mid-term break.

Unfortunately for us, we hadn't seen this coming, our minds having been superstewed by all the nonsense of recent happening; therefore, we had absolutely no say in what was to become of us.

Our Granda P, Momsie's dad, was a true one-off in every sense. He was his own man. He did what he wanted, when he wanted, and in whatever manner he wanted. For as long as we could remember, Granda P gave people the impression that he didn't care very much about them. In fact, it seemed he didn't care much for the world in general, and people in particular.

On the rare occasion that Granda P came visiting us, he would always drive down in an old jalopy, as

Momsie liked to call whatever vehicle of a two or four-wheel variety he was near the end of restoring. His favourite two-wheeler, and mine, was a vintage Norton motor bike which roared and rattled and whizzed and banged but which flew like the wind and swept you away to distant places, over land and in your head. It was truly indeed, a genuine Dream Machine.

Fortunately for us, being discharged into the incapable hands of Granda P, wasn't so terribly bad. Don't get me wrong: it wasn't that he was incapable of looking after us, his three grandchildren; no, he was the most capable man I knew, to his own fashion. It wasn't that he wasn't capable of running Gooseberry Farm, a farm that God knows how many preceding generations had been lumbered with. No, it was definitely in his blood, and he made sure it stayed there. It was just that Granda P was incapable of overcaring about how others considered him . . . well . . . incapable, I suppose!

And, although it was all very last minute, in terms of preparing to go, Tom and my surreptitious self did manage to include a few of our own items in the miscellaneous case for everything other than clothes and other personal effects to be worn, such as schoolbooks. Needless to say, amongst many items of a dubious nature was included a large stash of liquorice bubble gum, some party balloons, and our very own canister of nitrous oxide. Yippee! We had plans, big plans, and ones we had great hope of putting into effect away from the stifling supervision of parental worry and under the auspices of grandparental assistance.

In this respect, Granda P was absent-mindedly marvellous. Always, in the past, when we had been dumped into his lap in Gooseberry Farm, he had taken the approach that we weren't there, except when he wanted us to be there. We did exist – but outside the realms of his existence. We were his responsibility, but he wasn't responsible for whatever we got up to. It was a brilliant arrangement for all concerned, so long as there was nothing to be concerned about.

Gooseberry Farm didn't get its name from nowhere; in fact, you mightn't be far wrong in thinking that at one stage at least, the whole farm must have been involved in the production of nothing but gooseberries.

Granda P certainly did his level best to carry on the name of his homestead because everything about the place was connected in some way, shape or form to gooseberries. Gooseberry-scented candles of varying shapes and sizes for every occasion. Okay, we could hack this. Gooseberry soap in every sink. Okay, too, we could handle this. But gooseberry lemonade; gooseberry pie, tart, fool, crumble; and, of course, tons and tons of sticky gooseberry jam, wounded our taste buds with their sharp, tangy, bitter flavour.

I remember once when Tom and my inquisitive self plucked up the courage and asked Granda P why gooseberries, why did he produce and reduce so many? His answer was, 'I hate the damn things in their natural state, but they're wonderful blended into something else. They remind me of your granny, too!'

You see, many moons before, when I was only half the age I am, Granny P upped and awayed and left Granda, and she didn't disappear on her own. She headed off with a man a lot younger than her – her "toy-boy with a toupee" as Granda P determined him – and they settled together in the holiday villa she and Granda P owned in Deja, in the northern reaches of the sunny isle of Majorca. Even at a very young age, the three of us could see how much Granda P missed his villa; he really loved that place.

We weren't allowed to talk about it, certainly not within earshot of Momsie, and we could understand why; well, it isn't natural, is it? Therefore, since it wasn't talked about in our house, it wasn't talked about at all, because that's just the way it was.

The dust had long since settled on all the heave-ho associated with the split-up, and although Momsie occasionally did receive long distance phone calls that took her into an empty room with the door firmly closed behind, it didn't seem to make the slightest difference to Granda P or Gooseberry House. His home took on a friendlier, more child-welcoming appearance whereby it couldn't really be said to be untidy or dirty, rather that this special blend of dusty and looking ill-kempt was one and the same as Granda's look. Everything was where he wanted it to be, which, if you think about it, is where everything really should be. However, this isn't always where you'd *expect* it to be when you'd go looking for it.

This was the logic Granda P dwelt amongst, and it worked. Well, it must have worked for him because every time we saw him he seemed to be thriving, despite the best efforts of the world around.

'Sending them off to live with a seventy-year-old boy . . .' Dad had shaken his head and tutted away to himself, and this was by way of saying goodbye to the three of us.

Momsie, on the other hand, spent her last moments on the platform at the railway station explaining all her do's and don'ts in great detail, not that any of us were listening. Our minds were much too busy away off in the beyondness of what was going to be, what surely must be, another wonderful, wacky week of complete adventure and freedom. In the end-up, we were glad to be off, to be away, and to see what excitement lay at the end of our long train journey down to the coast.

Travelling by train is terrific, and we all enjoyed nearly every moment of it snaking its way down to Granda's beachy part of the country with its coasting way of life. It was like having our own big television screen where we could watch a lot of goings-on in back gardens and houses, in cars and shops, in lorries and factories, in prams, and people going about their lives as normal. But every time I saw a person with a certain newspaper in his or her hand, I wondered was Momsie inside it, I wondered what they would see, and I wondered what they would make of what they saw.

However, the further away from home we chugged and puffed and squealed and screeched and hooted and chikkety, chikkety, chikkety, chikketied along, the further we were removed from home and so the less we thought about it. And by the time we had set forth from our fourth station, all thinking was completely removed from behind and focused now on what lay ahead.

It was the midday train we had departed on, and so we had been up early to enjoy our good feed of Momsie's chocolate porridge; this was one thing we were definitely going to miss, there was absolutely no doubt about that. It wasn't beyond the realms of human possibility, however, that Granda P would come up with something just as interesting and tasty, although perhaps not quite as fulfilling.

At journey's end, there he was, on his own, apart from a very old station porter, all smiles and hugs and 'How are you?' and 'Great to see you!' And we knew he really meant it, every bit of it and more. Unfortunately, Granda P had chosen to bring along his favourite form of transport on good days, his all-white, convertible Beetle, with the hood down, of course. White bodywork, white canvas hood, white leather interior, white steering wheel, even whitewall tyres. Brilliant, except neither Tom nor my squashed self could see out in front of us because of the stack of cases piled up from our knees.

'Do you remember her name?'

Granda P was of course talking about his car. However, there seemed little point in either of the two of us in the back seat trying to join in, for we'd only be talking to ourselves. We could hear, though.

'Snowdrop!' Siobhan was in her element, sitting up front in such a handsome beast of a beautiful machine.

'Because . . .' Granda came alive with company, certainly every time we joined him.

'Because she hides herself all through the winter, but as soon as Spring comes . . .'

And with that, Granda P played a little tune with the car horn, and this he repeated every so often after. I don't know why he did this; I can only guess he must have passed a lot of people he knew. I was too busy studying the run of the creases in the leather of the suitcases!

And then, in the middle of our enjoyment, in the middle of all our enjoyment, it hit me, it hit us, all of us.

Wooooof! The most horrible smell in the world was concentrated in the countryside surrounding Gooseberry Farm.

'That's a terrible pong, Granda. What is it?' Siobhan was now paying the price of being up front and enjoying the openness of sky above.

Tom and my scrunched self were somewhat protected from the true strength of malodorous wiff all around by our wall of cases, but not for long. Our nostrils still had to draw air in from around and by now it was all much of a pongy muchness, and our faces screwed themselves up in disgust at our airy surrounds.

I caught a quick glimpse, in the rear-view mirror, of Granda P's nose twitching about as it caught the true value of what was unmissably there, in the breeziness we drove through.

'Smells to me like pig slurry. Farmer Fielding has leased some of the fields from me and I reckon it's pig slop he's spreading. With any luck, a good shower will have it washed in by teatime, although I don't think there's much luck on the horizon today.'

This last bit Granda P whispered, but we still heard him, even with the distinctive rattle of the Beetle engine behind us. As soon as he stopped talking, the full ferocity of the pingiest pong we had ever suffered, first of all swept over us and then, once it was satisfied it had cornered its victims, it rushed in and through us. Granda P seemed oblivious to it all.

'Cow slurry isn't so bad, not in comparative terms.

You wouldn't mind it so much. In fact, they say it does you a power of good to have your sense of smell woken up by something strong every so often.'

This time, in the tiniest of gaps between the cases, I caught what looked like more than just the hint of Granda P enjoying the stink of what we were going through. As soon as we stopped, with cases flung forward before us, Tom and my fervent self were clambering up and out over the sides of the vehicle and heading for the front door of Gooseberry House.

'Inside quickly and make sure it doesn't follow!' I followed on Tom's heels, in through the front door like a double flash. Siobhan quickly came after, and she opened the door and closed it immediately, every time Granda P lifted in a case. At least now we were able to breathe, to savour air of a quality that was fit to be drawn in through our nostrils and fill our lungs. What a relief!

'Granda, you must have forgotten to lock your front door when you left to collect us.'

Tom looked smilingly pleased with himself, not alone for having caught onto this, but for being able to share it with Granda. My eyes followed the line of Tom's words round to catch what was coming back from Granda.

'Lock doors? Why would I do that?' Granda P seemed mildly amused, but he must have noticed a different look returning from our faces. 'Sometimes I do, at night, when I remember, before I go to bed.' The smile he stuck on at the end was about as real as his words.

A triple shiver of concern ran up and down three spines as he spoke. We didn't like the sound of this.

13 GOOSEBERRY HOUSE

Granda P may have neglected the actual farming functions of Gooseberry Farm but Gooseberry House and its immediate surrounds, especially some of the barns and stables, had the look of care still about them.

Gooseberry House itself had always been a happy place for us, and, no doubt, for any and all who were lucky enough to be invited in to partake of its intrinsic goodness. Granda P was most definitely the biggest part of all that was wonderful here, but this feeling was also in the essence of the whole belong of the house.

On the outside, the house looked exactly right. With brickwork having popped its fine finish in some places, needing re-pointed in others. Windows re-puttied sometime long ago, all cracked now, having given up most essential oils, still awaiting an undercoat, not to mention a glossy overcoat. A beautifully tiled roof, Rosemary tiles, large near the eaves, small near the apex, many of whose smooth, man-made surfaces had exploded with the frosts of yesteryear, and which had taken to covering their exposed selves with green modesties of moss.

The curvature of water-butts relieving the vertical aspect of each corner of the house, and charged with the important job of collecting rainwater, but no longer able to hold too much because of the angular strain the stresses of time had put on the metal bands of their hold. Downspouts that cut their own angle on the world of roof water relocation. Guttering that wanted to have growth, that thought itself too good just to channel water along, that aspired to the greatnesses of window boxes.

And then there were the gardens. Lawns that had given up pretending, not to mention wanting, to be grassy areas of smooth contentment. Plants and flowers that in another place might have been denounced as weeds, and culled by poison or by decapitation, were happy here because they were perfectly suited to where they stood and didn't look out of place, even if a loner or two decided that the middle of a gravelly path was for them. It all looked perfectly natural, because it all was perfectly normal, in an unpretentious, unsophisticated, spontaneous kind of way.

Gooseberry House oozed contentment. It was happy with what it was, with who it was. It was more than satisfied with its lot in life. You could even go so far as to say that it was pleased with what it had achieved, and now it spent its time trying to improve the lot of those who came into contact with it. It had long established both who and what it was and desired nothing more than to be left to its own devices and stay settled in the world it was in, for, encapsulated in its hold was truth and meaning enough to help the three of us angle our own pitch at the world.

The first thing you noticed on entering Gooseberry House was that it smelt just right, and this took in everything from the mustiness of certain corners of some rooms to the uplifting hale of hyacinth plants with their bell-shaped, six-parted flowers of differing colours in the same-smelling downstairs rooms.

Then there were the rectangular and square and squarangular patches of darkness on every wall. It didn't matter whether the wall was painted or papered, there were these very obvious marks on them, where pictures and paintings had disappeared from. Somehow, though, they fitted in. To us, these were a constant reminder of Granny: she had taken them with her to her little island retreat off the coast of Spain. I don't know what they meant to Granda P; probably a lot more than he let on, certainly a lot more than we could tell.

Nothing in Granda's house matched, probably because it didn't need to: that's the way the place was, it's the way it had been, it's the way it would always be; because it's the way Granda P was.

The carpets throughout the house were a mishmash of different colours, different shades, different patterns, and it all seemed to work in the way a mosaic works. The stairs, especially, were an absolute delight to the eyes, and every time you ran up or down them, you felt you were a part of something wonderfully creative, ingenious, inspired, and stimulating in a visionary way. We could never say this about our stairs at home, or those anywhere else, for that matter.

The kitchen was relatively normal. It was as it must

have been when the house was first built, with more beautiful pieces of free-standing pine furniture added here and there. However, there weren't two of the ten chairs around the massive table the same, and that's the way it should be because as Granda P once told us, 'There are no two people who sit on them the same!'

In the bathroom and toilet, absolutely nothing matched! Toilet seats were a different colour to cisterns, pedestals at variance with sinks. And the wall tiles, well, they were a complete delight. You could sit on the toilet seat for ages and every time you moved your head, even slightly, you saw a different picture. It could be anything from cubism to futurism to surrealism to expressionism; in fact, you name it, if you looked carefully enough, every modern style of art was represented on Granda P's toilet or bathroom wall. In the bathroom, his *pièce de résistance* was the enormous brass bath, and Granda P took great pride and delight whenever he polished the outside of it; for this purpose, he used HP sauce, and it worked wonders. The inside of the bath was much easier cleaned: he used Steradent tablets, and they brought it up a treat.

Throughout the house, from landing to hall, from lounge to study and drawing room, Granda P's one extravagance was most obvious to behold – chandeliers. Nothing but the finest of cuts of the best of crystal shone out an inordinate amount of light from an immoderate number of light bulbs. Truly magnificent! *C'est magnifique*!

As soon as the cases were plonked into two bedrooms, it was straight down to the kitchen table to the delight of our taste buds, the entertainment of our salivary juices, and the fullness of our stomachs, as we devoured a strange mix of foods Granda P had pre-prepared. It was a conglomeration of bananas, hard-boiled eggs, tomatoes, cold baked beans, mince and fried potatoes – yummy-yummy scrumptious food, especially when you're starving with hunger.

'So, is everything okay with your mum and dad at home?' Granda certainly didn't mince his words.

We didn't know what to say. Eyes looked at eyes looking at eyes, and it was clear and obvious Granda P knew more than we did, otherwise he wouldn't have been so blatant in his asking. Silence held sway over our lips and, in as much as we could manage it, over our looks.

Thankfully, Granda P was on the move, and away from us, shrugging and twitching to himself and not hanging around either to catch a visual response from us or for us to hear the finish of what he said. But our wonder was far off and a great distance from where we were, way beyond Granda P and his blatherings; for inside our heads was firmly focused on the happenings of home. We knew we couldn't dwell on this, and anyway, whatever was happening would happen whether we thought about it or not.

'The first thing you can do to help is clear that sinkful of pots and pans.' Granda was setting out his store straight away. If this was a holiday, it would be a working holiday. 'I've worn the scouring brush down to a frazzle. I've knackered three Brillo pads, and I still can't manage to shift the glar on the inside of those pots and pans. The frying pan's the same except it has more stuck to the outside than the inside!'

By now, as Tom and my unsure self looked on, Siobhan was poking and scraping with a knife at the insides of one of the pots. 'What is it? What on earth have you stuck to the inside of this?' Her glance didn't shift from the interior of the pot, a bit like whatever it was she was hoking and poking at.

'Scrambled egg mainly, although some of it was a lot more than scrambled.'

Granda P headed for the kitchen door, as he sought to leave us alone to deal with the aftermath of past attempts of his to reinvent the shelled contents of nature's excellent little creations.

'Scrambled egg?' There wasn't much belief in Siobhan's reiteration of what Granda P had told us.

'Scrambled, boiled, poached, fried, plus whatever else you do with hen's effortless layings.' His words seemed to find their own way into our hearing, just as we were going to have to find our own means of dealing with his mess.

We were left to our own devices. We knew there was nothing new in this in our dealings with Granda P, just as we also knew it was a kind of test which we had to pass.

There was a lot of silence hanging about in the kitchen, apart from the noise Tom and my inquisitive self made while seeking here, searching there, in presses and in drawers, to see if there was anything, anything at all, that might help us in our challenge. There was nothing, certainly nothing we knew that would help.

'Right, let's hit Dinkydoo beach!' Siobhan was already turned and heading out of the kitchen.

'And how is that going to help?' Tom very kindly put words to my thoughts.

'Seaweed.' Siobhan sounded very sure of herself.

'What?' I hadn't a clue what she was saying.

'We'll gather some seaweed and when we boil this up in the affected pots and pans, they should sparkle to our liking.' Her smile convinced me she knew what she was saying, and I wasn't going to argue with any of this.

The three of us headed out into the great pong of the outdoors, and it wasn't long before we soon gave up trying to breathe through our sleeves. Instead, we playfully jostled our journey down the short distance to the coast and here we were surprised to find that Dinkydoo beach was far from empty. It appeared to be some sort of a social haven for couples of all ages, as well as people without people, and people with dogs.

It was a surprisingly social scene, and one we hadn't expected to come upon. This was added to in great measure by the wonderful sounds of the waves breaking and crashing and throwing themselves tirelessly upon the sandy shore, music that washed through the sounds of all else.

So, we trawled the shoreline, along the length of high-water line where, not so long before, handy-sized bundles of seaweed had deposited themselves for a well earned sandy rest, until the next high tide returned them to the industry of their work amongst the doings of the waves and the washings of the sea.

An armful each we gathered, and then we looked at each other because we hadn't a clue how much we would or wouldn't need. A second armful was gathered in under the grab of each other arm, and smiles led us off into laughter that was always the reckon of our togetherness at play; and so we ended up hunkered over, kneeling amongst the sea wrack, while trying to grab into our possession as much of it as we possibly could.

Roaring with laughter we were, as we tried to find our feet to follow out the way we had come in. It took a peculiar feat of physical engineering to enable us to walk, tri-stepping along together, leaning in to the support of another and another, so we could stagger off the beach and be gone homewards.

It seemed a longer way up we had to traipse on the return journey to Gooseberry Farm, with its great, big leany barn cum workshop to pass first before we reached the house.

Very seldom, if ever, were we invited into the gargantuan interior of Granda P's workshop in the barn. Normally, while stopping over at Gooseberry House, we sought out every excuse under the sun to find a reason to be inside the cavernous interior of what had definitely started off life as a barn and ended up becoming something else completely – namely, an incubator for initial ideas; a home to many good ideas that hadn't seen themselves through to completion yet; as well as a resting place for what undoubtedly were good ideas that had passed their forget-by date.

I remember Granda P once telling me that every *good* idea needs time and space for its process to progress if it is ever to become a *great* idea. I don't know what this meant in particular, but I had a fair idea what he was getting at in general. He obviously saw what was going on inside my head because he went on to say that he needed to keep some room inside his head for thoughts to expand and develop, in the same way as he needed a big working space to let the practical side of things take shape.

The strange thing is, a small but intense part of my head was always located there, inside his workshop, even when we weren't anywhere near the place. So, whenever we'd be chatting on the phone, my first question was always the same, 'Tell me, what are you working on now, Granda?' And I always got the same answer back, 'The best, the most brilliant, most technologically advanced motor vehicle in the world!' Or words to that effect, for it wasn't easy to quote Granda P because he sometimes used so many long-winded words that are far from popular in the modern vernacular.

However, no matter what angle of the leany old wooden barn Siobhan, Tom and my inquisitive self peeped in through gaps, gouges, splits, and even knotholes in the wood, we couldn't make out anything remotely connected to the outline of any type of a motor car that we knew.

'What do you think is in there?' Siobhan looked as though her face had melted into the obstruction of wood in front of us.

I tried to press my nozzle right in through a crack in the wood. It got stuck. I got stuck. I didn't want to appear a plonker by crying out for help. I didn't want to lose one of my permanent features, especially one I hand picked myself, every day. I couldn't get my hands in to help me out. I couldn't get my fingertips in to ease my predicament. As a last resort, I sucked in my cheeks and pulled in a quantity of air through my nostrils so they slimmed down to half their size, and this way I was able to extricate myself from my pickle. Only now did I notice Siobhan and Tom bent double in silent laughter.

'We thought you were stuck there for good!' This was about all my now guffawing sister could manage to say.

'Yeah, I thought I was going to have to get Granda P to let us into the barn so he could hammer your nose back out!' Poor Tom nearly fell over himself then with the level of hilarious merriment and tittering amusement rising up through him.

The two of them were still giggling to themselves and chuckling to each other as we made our way back over towards Gooseberry House and away from the carnivorous barn that tried to eat my nose. It was a strange world we lived in. It surely was.

On the way back into the house, we agreed between ourselves that we should ask Granda P about the contents of the barn. Siobhan and Tom needed to gloat and so they decided to pick on me in my moment of weakness, agreeing with each other that I was the one who should ask. I was in no position to deny them their desire, even though they obviously wanted to rub my nose in it.

And so, right as soon as we got back and got stuck into the boiling up of seaweed inside the filthy pots, I asked.

'Granda, we've been peering into your workshop from every angle . . .' Here, I looked up from my attacking scrub on the inside of a particularly mingy pan, the strange-smelling steam of seaweed and goo half amusing, half abusing, my nostrils.

It was no good; Granda P wasn't biting. In fact, he kept his nose to the point of what he was doing, showing he wasn't giving up on something so meaningfully important for the sake of six pokey eyes intent on something that was glaringly none of their business.

Siobhan encouraged me on with her look. Tom was intensely interested in the scrape and scrub of the exterior of the frying pan he was working on.

'No matter what time of day, no matter what angle the streaming shafts of light brighten up the inside, we can't manage to pick out the shape of the motor you've been working on for so long . . .' I stalled here long enough to ensure Granda P was listening to me. I knew he was still alive because he was still marvelling at the interior of the first pot we had finished.

'Is that so?' There was almost a twinkle of interest in Granda's voice, and I could nearly say he was pleased at the interest we had shown in him, at this aspect of himself that remained hidden from most others.

I tried to hold his attention in my smile. I tried to contain the new beginnings of a deep and lasting and wonderful and friendly relationship in that simple catch of the eye. Now I had made a start, I wasn't going to give up so easily, and so I didn't.

'Is it over by the front of the barn, near the double doors, or by the far side entrance?'

The three of us, having by now stopped what we were doing almost as much in protest as in interest, awaited a result from our curiosity about Granda's mechanical doings.

'Or maybe it's sitting in the same place for so long along the far side of your workshop that it's the reason why the whole structure leans down to the sea?' A slightly weakened smile broke on my face. I knew I had been a bit cheeky, more in the way I said it rather than in what I had actually said; but I didn't think I had been too audacious.

Tom looked at me. He gave no indication of what might have been what, before he, too, added to my measure. 'Maybe we could go in and see it sometime, Granda?'

I had never before heard Tom sound so plausible. I had never before witnessed so wily a smile catch hold of his facial muscles, until then. *Jeepers, there's a lot more to you than meets the eye!* I thought to myself.

Almost immediately after this, Granda P finished what he was doing, drew himself out to the fullness of his form and said enough to brighten the rest of our mid-term break with him.

'The engine's due back soon. Maybe even tomorrow.'

Excitement rose up through my veins until it was bubbling out of every aspect of me, and over at two similarly enthralled bodies. We were totally captivated by what Granda P had said, were completely taken by what this meant to us, for us. I knew I was not alone in having a mind that was bursting with the enthusiasm of wanting to see at first hand this magnificent vehicle.

'Can we see it, Granda?'

I was right up in front of him, trying not to pull him away from where he was, but wanting him, needing him, to respond now, quickly, quickly, quickly.

'Of course you can see her, as soon as she's done.'

Granda P made to turn away, to turn back to his own business, on his own, because that was what he was used doing. He was obviously willing to forget about what was so wonderfully important to his three grandchildren here, now, as we stood silently pleading our case with our eyes.

'But can't we just have a little glimpse of her now, just to see what she's like, to see the great job you've done so far?'

Siobhan added her own ample measure to our pleas. And by the time she had finished, the three of us were virtually on top of him, so strong was our urge to see, to know, to share in this amazing invention, for it couldn't possibly be anything else.

Granda P was undoubtedly a man well used to making his own decisions, for his own reasons, in his own timescale, for his own outcome, but eventually, and to a great cheer of delight from the three of us, he said 'Yes', and what's more, he did a very unadult-like thing – he acted on this straight away. And off we went, following along in Granda's word, as well as his footsteps.

'She was a special edition when she left the Wolfsburg factory, long before any of you were born. I've added my own extras to their extras and now she's a complete one-off; there couldn't possibly be another of its ilk in the world!'

By now we were eagerly helping heave open the broad fit of one of the barn's double doors. I could feel a great sparkle of excitement catch me inside and fizzle up through my veins until my mind was buzzing with elation. I had to stop myself from becoming all laughy and giggly with the quickening of emotions and the slowing of our pace.

It needed all our might to encourage the door off its rusty anchorage and into the swing of an arc it hadn't known in a very long time. With four bodies ramming as much bodily shove, haul, push, jostle and thrust into it, we persuaded this relic of a door to travel only half the distance it should have done.

'Here, open up this other door as well and you'll stand a better chance of seeing what's what.' It took us nearly ten minutes – armed with a spade, a hammer, and a pint of oil – to convince the door, that hadn't been darkened in God knows how long, to open up fully for us.

The three of us gawked around in near disbelief.

My neck craned all along the yawning stretch of massive oak beams holding up the roof. I had been in a lot smaller churches than this; we all had. For what had seemed massive on the outside, truly gave the term a new meaning on the inside.

Above a certain height over our heads, there was a vast emptiness of space because nearly everything that was in there resided on the ground: old tractors, farm machinery, bits of boats, a couple of motor cycles, even an enormous wicker basket that could only have been used for transporting elephants in.

It was awesome.

Awe-inspiring.

In a stunningly breathtaking sense.

And even greater wonders awaited us.

14 THE ORANGEMOBILE

Granda P led our parade into the eerie silence of barnormous expanse. There should have been a band playing in our procession, but the stillness of the air inside didn't seem to allow for such. Instead, it held a quiet, gentle hush over the proceedings, which became a total hush when Granda's steps called us to a halt.

'I've recalibrated and restructured everything to take account of the improved thrust from the three-litre Porsche engine that's being rebuilt at a specialist marine workshop just down the coast; they're almost friends now, they've helped me out so much.'

Granda might well have continued to talk, but I wasn't listening, not fully, not half, hardly at all. My head was full of one word and one word only: Porsche. It conjured up a whole world of fast cars, rally winners, with their engines at the back. I knew a little about these German cars and their fantastic racing pedigree, and a beautiful picture of one kept flashing before my eyes inside my head.

'I hope it's a red one!'

There, I had gone and blurted out my thoughts, again. I had gone ahead and said what I was thinking without account of what was being said or thought around me. And why not? Why shouldn't I say what was on my mind? It was only but right I should share my innermost feelings of good and joy with the others, even though I didn't hear a peep from any one of them.

The whole barn seemed to fill up very quickly again with silence, until Granda P broke the spell.

'She's orange!'

What? An orange racing car? What were they thinking of – advertising oranges? Yuk! Orange? Orange or green would have been the last two colours I would have chosen for any car, a racer or not. It was beyond my comprehension why anyone would want to spoil the magnificent looks of such a beautifully crafted sports car with the reddish-yellow rind colour of a globose juicy pulped fruit! Someone at the factory must have suffered a little moment of madness when he gave the order to splash the outside of such a glorious machine with such a completely gaudy colour.

Ah well, the optimist in me accredited it with the fact that it was definitely a one-off: there would not be another of its like in the whole country, the whole world, I hoped!

'Beautiful bright orange, with an off-white, creamy-coloured piping along the edges. And the roof's creamy coloured as well. And there's lots of chrome: chrome hubs on the wheels, chrome . . .'

I didn't want to hear any more. I couldn't take any

more, because I couldn't think what this looked like; it certainly didn't seem like any Porsche I knew. All I could think was that Granda P had taken leave of his senses. Poor Granda. And I knew what must have happened him: I'll bet it was all the years of drinking the water pumped up from his well; yes, that must be it! Dad always said it tasted of iron and if you drank it all the time it would rust your brain. Poor Granda.

By now we were in the middle of the workshop area of the barn and Granda P had stopped alongside a great big green canvas awning covering what looked like another giant wicker basket thereunder. *This couldn't possibly be his Porsche; he must have two, one stacked on top of the other* was all I could think – or was the iron in the water starting to affect *my* brain? It was milk for me from now on!

My mind eased when the picture of a big, car workshop-type elevation machine came into my head; yes, Granda P must have installed some sort of mechanism like this in the recent past so he could work on the underside of his vehicle.

'One stand at each corner and we'll fold the tarpaulin off together. Okay?'

At the same time as he was speaking, Granda P was motioning and gesturing with his hands for whoever to go wherever and do whatever, together.

This all seemed to register properly within Tom and Siobhan's heads and bodies, for they both gave their agreement in a form that was audible, understandable and acted on immediately. My head, my brain, my mouth, was still stuffed with iron and orange; it was impossible for me to get anything out other than a tinny pip. But I soon saw where I wasn't and I had enough sense to fill the missing position, while Granda P took up the challenge of my understanding again.

'The brakes are disc all round, ventilated, of course. Remember, it's just as important to be able to stop in a hurry as it is to take off in haste. Nought to sixty should register in around seven seconds, but we'll not know until we try her out properly.'

This last piece of information was whispered as an aside to us, kind of top secret, if you know what I mean, and had the effect of making me look around to see if we were being spied upon.

'Okay. Is everybody ready? Right, then, on my count of three, take a deep breath, squint your eyes, and fold her forward towards me. One, two, three . . .'

I neglected to understand quickly enough the meaning implied behind Granda's first two points in his set of instructions. Therefore, I swallowed a large amount of dust and other tasteless particles of debris thrown into the air by our shifting of the tarpaulin. My eyeballs acted as magnets for some of the bigger shards momentarily made homeless. So, while I coughed and spluttered and rubbed the dirt further into the watering of my eyes, I heard Siobhan and Tom's gasps and gulps and exclamations at the wonder and beauty of what they beheld.

'Cor, she's stunning, magnificent, splendid! What a beautiful big beast!'

These last few words, coming from the deeper

voiced of the two, couldn't make it into the settle of my thoughts. My mind couldn't square what was said with the glorious lines of remember in my head of the dazzlingly attractive form of a Porsche 911, even if it was discoloured orange. By now, too, I had rubbed enough to have worn out a good proportion of the corneas of my sight. And when finally I did manage to fix focus on, and then visually define, what my eyes were taking into the understanding of my brain, I was stutteringly lost for words.

'It's . . . it's a . . . it's a Type Two . . . it's a Volkswagen Type Two . . . it's a Type Two Volkswagen Campervan . . . and it's orange!'

Of course it was orange; I couldn't miss what I already knew, which was that it was very definitely the colour of the peel of a rounded citrus fruit; it was orange. As if it wasn't real, the three of us were straight over and touching it and watching Granda P at the same time to make sure that what we were doing was all right by him.

'Of course, go on, enjoy it. Have a look at the interior and see if it conforms to your expectations. And by the way, it's only orange on the outside; it's sky blue underneath.'

Our attentions were solely on the orangemobile and so we didn't pay much attention to Granda P's words. His actions were different, though, because now he was nodding us over, shooing us forward with the motion of his hands and head. This was all the encouragement we needed. In an instant, chrome handles were pressed in and as soon as doors slid and swung open, our trio of breaths were taken away from us.

'Wow!'

'Whao!'

'Woo!'

This was all we could articulate. Coherent, intelligent thoughts compressing themselves into words just wasn't possible. We were dummies, struck dumb by the splendour and excellence of what we beheld. We knew we were in a new dimension. We could sense this was above and beyond anything we had ever come into contact with in our mediocre lives so far.

This was, indeed, no ordinary Volkswagen. And let me tell you, where we came from in this life, we were experts on mediocre cars, and what this brings, in aspirational terms at least, is a wanton knowledge of every marvellous super car there is on the road. What Granda P had built was total, utter, unadulterated luxury of the kind only found in magazines and swanky television stories. Never before had we had first-hand contact with something so absorbingly brilliant, something so phantasmagorically superb.

As I climbed in, I noticed the door seals were of a much superior quality to anything I had come across yet in my life. My hands then sunk into a soft sumptuousness in the feast of leather inside. My mind was momentarily dislocated inside this luxuriance of feel, this magnificence of quality in workmanship, as well as in the totality of perfection. An absoluteness of excellence was all around.

This was most definitely no Volkswagen-finished interior, special edition or not. In fact, this was work of a more exacting standard than even renowned customisers Karmann could have delivered. It was skill and craftsmanship of a level that only comes when love and understanding, time and patience, are involved, and when both of these boths are blessed with the intelligence evident only after decades of learning and doing.

There was no doubting this was Granda's artistry, his *pièce de résistance*, the sum total of all his labours of love: it was his life's work. With this understanding now in me, I could feel a deep emotion swell up within, because I felt so proud of my Granda P and the beauty and excellence of what he had achieved.

'Cor, look at that! What are all those for, Granda?'

As soon as my vision caught sight of the mountings on the front dashboard – all the switches and knobs, all the dials and levers – a very different emotion exploded quickly through me. I leapt forward and into the driver's seat. My hands clamped onto the magnetic hold of the steering wheel, even though it was just a plain, old-fashioned, white, plasticky, steering wheel, obviously the original.

It was just as well my hands landed where they were, and just as well they stayed thereabouts for a matter of seconds because as soon as I lifted them off, as soon as they made to twiddle and twist and flick and pull at the whole range of gadgetry at arm's length, a voice boomed in from outside.

'Don't touch any of the controls!'

It was Granda's voice and it was a good thing he was so quick in his vocal recognition of what I was making my move to do. Three heads swung automatically round in the same quick-speed rotary response to catch exactly what was what.

'Don't flick any of the switches or press any of the buttons or pull any of the levers because . . . because they haven't been fully tested yet . . . and some that have been tested only work when she's in motion . . . and there are some that wouldn't be safe!'

Something registered inside me that Granda P mightn't be telling the full truth here. However, now seemed a less than appropriate time to challenge him on any of this.

'Of course I won't, Granda. I'll just press this instead.'

'Don't touch that!'

But he was too late.

15 LiFT OFF

I hit the round bit in the centre of the steering wheel, and I hit it a good hard slap with the thump of my hand, expecting a loud squeal of a squeaky noise to reverberate around the woody interior of the barn.

But no sound came from the horn: not a blast, not a blare, not a honk, not a hoot, not even a little toot. A sound did come from Granda P, however, and it was something along the lines of:

'Oh no!'

Whatever he thought would happen didn't happen, but only for about two or three seconds. Then, after a lot of clicking noises and a few pumping sounds, something stirred deep inside the campervan.

A rattling noise, a vibrating feeling, and then something caught my eye, and it was Siobhan move faster than I had ever seen her move before. As she shot out of the wagen, Tom flew off in hot pursuit. My own survival instincts were a few beats behind but in a flash, I, too, was standing, huddled in as close as I could get against my two siblings beside Granda.

By now the rattling and squeaking and pumping and creaking noises seemed to have taken hold of the whole vehicle, and now we could see something strange happening in the "up above" sense of what we were staring at.

'Sorry, Granda.'

It was all I could think of to say. It was as much as I *could* say. I was choking back tears of fear for the damage I had undoubtedly done to Granda's pride and joy – which I had finished off before he even had a chance to finish it.

'Don't worry, son. We'll now see whether my special invention is working or not.' A firm hand rubbed through my hair, and as I smiled a sad and sorry look up to him, he smiled back at me.

This lasted for only a matter of seconds because we had to return our attentions immediately to what was happening on the roof of the campervan. Before our very eyes, a ginormous yellow rubberiness of a balloon was rising up, up, up, to a size that dwarfed the wagen.

'Is it meant to be that big?' Tom gave voice to all our younger thoughts.

But Granda P's thoughts were elsewhere. 'Any moment now. Any moment now, she's going to lift up off the ground!'

We could hardly believe what we were hearing, and so our eyes glued all the more firmly to the look and study of what was happening in front of us. And still the vibrating, rattling, pumping din reverberated out, its incessant drone and hum and creak and rattle a worry to our wonder.

Then, with our very own eyes, we saw the campervan lift itself up off the floor of the barn. It was only a couple of inches, and then a few inches more, and then, with eyes agog and minds agone, the fullness of this massive vehicle was floating in mid-air, a couple of feet off the ground, right in front of us.

Just as suddenly as it had all started, the whole interior of Granda's cavernous workshop went quiet, absolutely hushed with silence; not a sound could be heard until a great crashing din frightened the lives out of all of us. Petrified beyond belief, the four of us jumped eight feet into the air, and it felt as if we stayed there a lot longer than the campervan had managed during its feat of flying.

In reality, though, perhaps our great leap was more internal than external. Either way, it had been caused by the van coming back down to earth with a sudden jolt, as a couple of tons of metalwork landed a bit too forthrightly upon itself.

'I knew she would do it! I knew I could do it!'

Granda P was now over trying to hug his oversized Volkswagen, while giving it slaps of *well done* as well.

What we had just seen, what we had just then been witness to, obviously amounted to a more than acceptable measure of success in Granda's mind. And so we breathed more easily, and smiled more generously, as we stepped stealthily forward to encourage Granda P to enjoy his success.

'Did you see it? Didn't you see it fly? Wasn't it amazing? Wasn't it truly brilliant?'

Granda P was now in the process of shaking our hands, and with not just a single-handed grasp on our reality, but double-handedly pursuing the pleasure of our pride.

'Yes, yes, it flew, up to about there.' Siobhan's hand marked the approximate distance off the ground.

As we watched this, we had to avert our gaze very quickly because of a sudden roar from ahead. The balloon that had stretched out to its full extension decided it had had enough of this showing off business and fell back down upon itself and into its restful, reduced position.

'Yes, well, a few of the finer details will have to be ironed out on paper. You three can help me there. Physics isn't all quantum leaps. Aristotle's physical treatises don't have all the answers. You have to work everything out for yourself as you go along in this life. That's the way everything works. Well, that's my theory, for what it's worth.' Granda then proceeded to carry out a few checks on the van.

'You're quite right.' Siobhan didn't sound so enthusiastic either in what she was saying or the way in which it was meant, but it did sound very self-righteous.

'I think you might need a compressor with greater capacity. Mind you, the one you have did remarkably well, considering there were a couple of doors left open.' As he finished his expressive piece of eloquence, Tom shared his imperious look with me, as if he was suggesting I was in some way to blame for this.

I wasn't about to share with him the knowledge that I knew I was. Anyway, there was no chance of me arguing against this quiet assertion, especially since Tom and physics went together like toast and marmalade.

'That's it. A bigger generator, and with all the hatches sealed, we'll take off for the heavens even with the extra load of an engine and four persons inside. Brilliant! And I think I'll change the procedure for starting this.' Granda P looked and sounded happy, really happy – really, really happy, even when he smiled his final thoughts in my direction.

The idea of this – the thought of a big lump of a car, a van really, taking off for the sky above – sent a wave of delight, mixed with a generous helping of excited fear, down the run of my spine. But then this was followed along by a thought flicking across my mind.

'There might be a way of making the campervan feel lighter . . .'

I knew what I was saying didn't sound right. Of course it didn't, because it wasn't what I wanted to say; it wasn't what I meant to say. It was perfectly obvious to me I didn't have the same science brain as Tom, especially now, when he would have had absolutely no bother saying what I had to say.

'What about if we connect a cylinder of helium up to the generator? It should provide a lighter mix of gas into the balloon, resulting in greater buoyancy for us. What do you think?'

My regard was flicking between Tom and Granda, focusing mainly on my brother, in the unsure and uncertain expectation he would pick up on some point I had incorrectly stated. My hope was that he would agree with me. My desire was that he would add to what I had said.

'That's certainly an interesting proposition. We'll have to look into that.' The knit of Granda's furrowed brow relaxed a bit but not quite enough to make me feel my suggestion had balanced the books for the early, and perhaps untimely, starting of his balloony experiment.

'It might just work. In fact, I'd go so far as to say that this is an inspired piece of scientific judgement. Well done!' Tom's really positive spin gave me great hope, especially when I saw Granda's head nod in positive approval.

'Okay, then, when the engine's been sorted out, we'll give it a go!' Granda P looked well pleased with this turn of events.

'Yeah, it'll be a good laugh if nothing else!' Siobhan's words may have been the truest spoken by any of us. At least we knew now we were going to find out.

The remainder of our time spent then, under Granda's close supervision in the workshop, was passed marvelling at the finer points of detail in the campervelle. However, the tendency now was to keep hands firmly tucked away inside pockets while we did so. None of us wanted a repeat performance, or worse, of the mischief my idle hands had earlier instigated. Ah well, that's how everyone learns, isn't it?

The rest of that day, evening time really, was passed absorbing all the fascinating stories and titbits Granda P deemed suitable to share with us about himself. He most definitely was one of the most exceptional of men, and well we knew how blessed we were to be in the share of such good company.

I wondered at myself for never before having noticed this about my granda. Yes, he had always been good fun to be with, fantastic fun sometimes when he really got going, but, as he talked and we listened, I realised this was also a man whom I actually liked.

This wasn't just in terms of him being a relation; no, it was through who he was inside himself rather than what he was, as others could see him. He had lived a wonderful life, done all sorts of different jobs in all sorts of different climates, in diverse parts of the world. But an underwhelming feeling of sorrow made itself apparent within me that Granny wasn't there now to share in it all with us: that would have made it all complete.

Everything Granda P told us had a special relevancy, not just to the campervelle but to a time and a place and a part of his life when he had been away somewhere exotic working. The exact type of work he was off doing was never properly specified, only sometimes alluded to, but I believe it had something important to do with the petroleum industry.

The real importance in all he told us always seemed to tie in with a certain aspect of the Volkswagen. For instance, it was when he was out hunting the deadliest of man-eating tigers in the wilds of one of the worst jungles in South-east Asia that Granda P developed the bulletproof tyres for his vehicle. "Deflation-proof" was what Granda P said his invention should really be called because it guarded against letting all the air out of a tyre spiked by a sharp stone or a snap of hardwood.

When Tom suggested he should have patented his idea all those years before and gone into business developing it with the military, Granda P would have none of it.

'No, that's not how we function. If you have an idea, it's only because you need to, and so you use it to your own advantage and the good of others. You don't waste your time with patents. And anyway, it was your father's recipe.'

This brought a stunned silence to the three faces in the full grip of his story.

'What, our dad invented a compound to bulletproof tyres?' Siobhan's mouth hung as open as her eyes; incredulity was staring out of her.

'Of course he did, he just didn't know it then, and do you know what's more? He still doesn't know it now!' Granda offered a cheeky big grin back to the catch of our expressions. He knew we needed to know more. But it was less than obvious to us whether we were going to hear any more.

'Your dad gave me some recipes for jungle cooking. Yuk! Indigestible, horrible stuff that wasn't safe to let anywhere near your mouth! So, the first time I made it, I had stopped to mend a puncture, my second of the day, and, not having another tyre or anything else worth using to hand, I slapped the stuff on the inside of the damaged tyre. Well, the laugh was on me because it worked a treat, a real treat. And since that day, I've cooked up that mix for every one of my tyres. Brilliant or what?' Granda's self-satisfied smile beamed all over us.

The three of us were too charmed by the idea of the whole thing to say anything, or do anything, other than nod in very distant agreement.

'That's amazing!' I thought something needed said, and this was all I could come up with that made any sense as my mind was still trying to grapple with the process of knowing what I didn't understand, as well as understanding what I didn't know.

'What about the windows?'

Tom gave a little look away from Granda P and over toward Siobhan and my still befuddled self as he asked his question. It sounded innocent enough, but I could tell there was a bit of drive underneath the surface of his words; it seemed he might be trying to scratch a different itch.

'Oh no, well, I don't think they're bulletproof but they're probably not far off it . . .'

Granda meant to continue but as he broke his flow for air and thought, Tom interrupted – and a bit too sharpishly for my liking.

'Oh, how's that, then?' It was more than obvious that Tom thought he was onto something here.

'Well, I reckoned if I ever managed to get her into the air that ordinary window glass mightn't do the trick. And so I relieved an old aeroplane of its high tensile panes of glass and cut them to size. Damned hard work it was, too, without the right equipment and having to make do!'

The expression on Granda's face was more than enough to put any and all notions of disbelief right out of our heads. This was real and made the story of Dad's concoction being cooked to fill up tyres all the more real, too; it certainly didn't sound concocted.

It's a serious business getting to know your granda, especially when what should have happened over years of daily nods and notice was squashed into days full of years of tell and tale. It was like a dream come true, for here, at last, not only had we come into close personal contact with our granda, but he turned out to be a complete revelation, a larger-than-life character. Plus, he had built one of the best vehicles known to man: so long as everything worked as it should and according to plan.

Somehow, the bitter pill of existence so far in life had taught me that the difference between success and tomfoolery is never exact or great enough for the one to eliminate all chances of the other.

And so, in a fanciful frame of mood, of feeling elevated but with both feet still firmly settled on the ground, we said our goodnights and headed up the windy, creaky staircase, to chase up every whisper of a dream ready to delight all inner consciousness.

16 DODGY DEALINGS

The next morning and it very quickly became apparent to us that Granda P had a habit – or what would have been termed and terminated at home "a bad habit" – and it was of sitting up into the early hours of the morn and definitely not tidying up after himself. Empty bags of crisps, empty packets of nuts, empty bottles of what must have been a local beer-type beverage, along with lord alone knows what other distractions, meant Granda P didn't get his newspaper crossword finished again.

Here, I must admit to a guilty thought arriving uninvited and unannounced inside my head and to the effect that perhaps we three were having this disabling effect on him. Poor Granda – perhaps he needed a bit more thinking time than normal after we had gone to bed.

There was still no sign of Granda P for as much of the morning as we were alive to, and so we got on with plenty of tidying and cleaning before Tom and my jaded self became bored with what we were doing and headed out into the rescue of the great outdoors.

Needless to say, we did have a particularly good lump

of liquorice bubble gum secreted between us to do with what we would.

So, by the time half an hour of our efforts had passed us by outside, we had a great big balloon of our own inflation readied and waiting, in anticipation of showing it off to Granda. While we had time to be extra ready, we stringed and tethered it to a bush, and watched its balloonyness dance around to the favours of a light wind while still managing to maintain contact with the telephone wire high above. Nothing at this time showed on the surface of the balloon because the line wasn't alive with the thoughts, tellings and sharings of any two from phone to phone.

Tom and my enthusiastic self couldn't wait to show Granda P our unpatented invention, which also happened to be courtesy of a by-product of Dad's delightful dabblings with foodables.

It was while stomping around outside, waiting for a very tardy Granda P to rise up from his theatre of inner dreams, that we heard the tyres of a big dieselly engine mulch up the gravel of the driveway as it made its hasty way up to the house.

'Tell them to drive round to the workshop. Open it up for them. I'll be down in a minute.' With that, Granda's smiling old head cuckooed back in through the window opening it had popped out of.

Tom and my spirited self sprinted off, told the three surly burlies in the white van what was what, before sprinting round to open up the barn for them. I didn't like the look of these three; in fact, I took an instant dislike to them, especially when, after reversing in under our guiding supervision, the three unshavens took off in thirty different directions, investigating and inspecting whatever came their dodgy way.

'What are you doing with this lot here?'

'We'll take this heap of junk off your hands – for a price, of course.'

'Tell the old fella we'll not charge him too much to clear out this rubbish for him.'

'Tell him yourself!'

The commanding bellow of Granda's voice was like a military officer happening in upon some lazy squaddies. Well, you wanted to see them straighten up straight away and slither back over toward the open tailgate of the white van.

'Is everything as it should be in here?'

I had never before noticed Granda P look so big, or sound so serious, as his features ate up the challenge of the three unsavouries. He was obviously well used to dealing with all sorts of dicey, distrustful and dubious characters.

'Yes, these gentlemen just expressed an interest in spending some money.' I laid it on a bit thick with my best country accent, especially when pronouncing the word *gentlemen*.

'Ah, did they now?' Granda then turned the full of his attention on the three buffoons, before adding, 'Where's Rogers and Peters? Can they no longer afford a bit of time away for an old hand like me?' Through the delivery of his words, Granda P conveyed the message that he was a bit miffed at not warranting the attentions of the bosses and having to make do with this lot.

'Not today, I'm afraid. They've got bigger fish to fry somewhere else up the country, I think. Called me up, said it was urgent. I thought to myself, must be going racing with a fine engine like this. But now I see the heap it's to go in, I can't understand what all the fuss and hurry was about.'

The gruffian who talked too much, and thought too little, then turned his head away from Granda P and offered a very unamusing nod and a wink and a stupid grin over toward his two compatriots. None of this was lost on any of the rest of us in the barn.

'Is that right, now?'

It was easy to see Granda P had the measure of him, of all three of them. It was obvious to us how he'd rather deal with them, but something stood in his way, and I reckoned it was the shifting and fitting of his engine. I think all thinking persons present were grateful for the veil of silence that came down upon proceedings then.

'Okay, if you're sure that's where you want it, we'll pop it in for you.' The beardy leader of the three certainly didn't have any hesitations about himself.

'I'll give you a hand.' Granda moved through his words in a conscious effort to get proceedings started.

'No, no, don't you bother an old body like yourself! We're better at it ourselves, aren't we, lads?' A wry smile caught the bemused faces of the other two. 'I tell you what, though: we could murder a cup of tea!'

Something unstated, but nonetheless suggested, lay behind the smile that followed; it caught my notice straight away and I didn't like the look of it one little bit.

Granda's eyes passed this request onto me, and although I wanted to put in a formal protest, I bit my tongue, said nothing, and left the three burlies to their heavy business, and Tom and Granda P to do their watching.

'Plenty of milk in mine!'

'Three sugars in them all!'

'Make sure it's real tea and not that powdery dust in those bags!'

I wanted to tell them to get stuffed. In fact, I wanted to tell them all to get stuffed, that I was no tea boy, but instead I legged it over to the house as fast as I could.

'Siobhan, Siobhan! Put the kettle on!'

My shouts filled every space in the high-ceilinged kitchen with my announcement, before shooting out the kitchen door and diminishing into the far corners of the house. If sis was in, she wasn't hearing. Or, if she was hearing, she wasn't listening. Or if she was listening, she certainly wasn't answering. I tried again, only this time from the deepest depths of my bellow.

'Siobhan, you're to make tea, strong tea, for those three delivery guys with Granda's engine!'

Before too long, Siobhan had done the necessary and I had a strong pot wet, tray set, back door toed open, and was on my way across to the barn, when I met Granda, Tom and two of the delivery blokes on their way back to the house; the third of their number being presently engaged in shifting the white van round to the front door.

'Where's all the biscuits, then, chum?'

One of the two nearly sent the tray flying from my arms when he followed up his question with a good, solid thump on my back, just as I was carefully turning to go back in with them. I hadn't been expecting this.

'Yeah, where's all the fancy chocolate cake and cookies?'

I tried to round on this second remark, on the silly smile of the other who was still busy nudging at his mate while chirping deliriously to himself, but I had too much to hold to effect it properly.

As soon as we were back in the kitchen, the two shifters made themselves at home at the table without even thinking about washing their hands. It was then I caught sight of the third, bearded member of this nefarious grouping make his way in through the hall, eyeing all as he went. He only popped his nose in through the doorway for a matter of seconds.

'I've a phone call to make. It'll only take a couple of seconds. Okay? Just need to check up on the next job.'

He didn't think it worth his while to show himself, with only his words making it into our presence. He obviously wasn't as dumb as the other two, who weren't capable of pretending they were anything else.

'Sure, go ahead!' As soon as Granda's words were out, the kitchen door was pulled firmly shut.

I set the tray down a bit too curtly on the table, gave Tom an awakening nudge with my elbow, and announced in as brazen a voice as I could muster, 'See to yourselves, guys; the biscuits are over there!'

Out the back door Tom and my apprehensive self shot, and round the side of the house to where our liquorice bubble gum balloon remained anchored to its airy inflated purpose alongside the telephone line. By the time we made it round, words were already showing and Harry here, at our end of the line, was conversing with someone with a speech impediment, judging by the mess of words and mistakes coming back the other way.

All we could make out was that his name was Enri, or something like that, for it was impossible to make out much of what he said clearly.

'I bet you he's French. He must be speaking with a French accent and his name is probably Henri – Henry!' Tom's whispers took me by surprise for I was in a different world trying to decipher what wasn't what. 'They're setting up a meeting, a rendezvous, and he's telling the Frenchman to bring the guns, and he'll bring the loot . . .'

'Yeah, but when?' Unfortunately, I turned away from what I was reading to look at Tom as he spoke.

'Leave coast tomorrow night. New job to do before then. Easy pickings, an old guy . . .'

'What are you two doing round here?'

The shock of a voice catching from behind us, unseen and unannounced, made us almost jump out of our skins, and so it took us a few seconds to realise who it was.

'Siobhan . . .' As soon as I said her name I knew I had announced it too loudly, but I couldn't help myself. 'What are you doing here?'

By the time I had finished my question, the great ease of knowing we weren't going to be shot in the back had entered my being. I could have hugged her, I was so happy to see her.

'What do you mean, what am I doing here? What are you two up to?' Siobhan stood smilingly awaiting a response. 'And, perhaps more to the point, what are you doing playing with a big balloon? And what's that written on it?'

Fearing the worst, that we might be overheard by the bearded leader of the delivery thugs, I advised her to *Ssssshhh!* Tom was a couple of steps ahead of me because he already had the balloon untethered and was bringing it rapidly down to earth.

'That's funny . . .' Siobhan stepped over to take a closer look at it. 'I could have sworn there was something written on the side of it.' She inspected the balloon all over, but it was a head-scratching mystery to her where all the wording had disappeared to. 'That's really strange. Ah well, it just must have been the reflection of something, Very strange, indeed.'

'Come on, we'd better head back in. I wouldn't want to leave three poor crooks on their own with Granda P for too long.' Tom led us off through the whisper of his words and round to the back of the house, where he tied the balloon onto a nice shiny camellia bush.

'What do you mean, crooks? I thought these were delivery men with Granda's new engine.' At least Siobhan now had the presence of mind to whisper her worries out to us.

'Not here, not now – we'll tell you all about it later.' I leant in toward Siobhan but at the same time turned my head away, in case anyone who might have been watching from inside was able to lip read.

As we entered through the back door, their leader, this bearded Harry guy, came in from the front hall at exactly the same time. Fortunately, he wasn't used to youthsters like us and so he didn't take us on – not the slightest bit of notice did he place on the fact that we all returned to the same place at the exact same time. Thank goodness he was a bit slow in his appraisal of the situation, because I don't know what lie I would have been able to make up on the spot.

'Right, gentlemen, a quick cup of the finest and we're off. So much to do, so little time to do it all in. And have you any monies you'd like me to pass onto Mr Rogers and Mr Peters for you?' A distastefully large grin slapped itself onto the frontal aspect of Harry the hood's facial hair.

It didn't work.

'You can tell them I'll be in to sort them out as soon as I have the engine connected up and running. I don't think my account will give them cause for concern; they know I'll not be leaving the country for the sake of a few pounds.' Granda smiled as enormously as the hold of his teeth would let him.

'Do you hear that, boys? Now why would anyone want to leave this beautiful coastline to go to a foreign one? Certainly not for the sake of a few pounds, eh?'

A gruff round of laughter caught hold of the three of them, and they laughed themselves up and off their chairs, out of the kitchen, through the hall, into their van, and they were still laughing as they churned up the gravel of the driveway.

Before they left, though, I noticed Granda P draw a £20 note from his pocket and lodge it surreptitiously into the driver's hand. A little nod passed between them at this point, and the burly Harry muttered about there being no need, that they would be well paid for their delivery today, before shoving it down and into the depths of his trouser pocket.

As soon as their white van had agitated gravel the whole length of the driveway and they had disappeared from view but not yet from hearing, Granda P spoke.

'I wouldn't trust those three as far as I could throw them!'

This was all he needed to say, and it certainly was all he had a chance to say before myself and Tom let Granda P and Siobhan in on what we knew.

'They're crooks, thieves, robbers, and they plan another job before meeting up with Henri, their French connection, tomorrow night, around midnight!' I had to struggle to get all this out in the one breath. I knew from the look on Tom's face that as soon as I stopped for air he would be ready to add his bit.

'Guns, they're doing a deal with this Frenchman, and they're getting guns in return . . . And I bet you I know where they're going to rob between now and then . . .'

Tom did manage to catch a quick breath in his roll of communication, but none of us knew he was finished because we were still waiting for him to tell us where and what and perhaps even when. We all stood quietly a bit longer than we should.

'Tell us!' Siobhan sounded as she looked – exasperated!

'Here! I reckon they're going to rob here!' Tom's assertion stopped us all in our tracks – inside our heads, at least.

Granda was the first to recoil from this mental assault. 'Why? What happened? Did you hear him say something when he was on the phone?' He looked more than slightly worried but a little under slightly shaken.

Tom and my doubting self looked at each other momentarily.

'Sort of.' In the split second before I said this, I already knew it would not be enough. Six eyes challenged me to continue.

'Stay here a moment and we'll show you.' I deliberately included Tom in my reckoning. I ran off round the back of the house and returned, seconds later, with a piece of string in my hand and an inflation of liquorice bubble gum playfully enjoying the fun of the air above.

'What in struth is that?' Granda was over sniffing up at its enormity of expansion, having the good sense not to want to touch it in case it exploded in his face.

'It's a by-product of one of Dad's "almost" inventions. But watch this!' I freed the great length of string from my hold and fed the balloon up toward the telephone wire above. Then I gave Tom the nod and off he skipped indoors.

Within seconds, Granda's jaw began to drop, drop, drop, as his mouth opened wider and wider and wider, until I thought he would never manage to properly close it again. At the same time, Siobhan's eyes opened wider and wider and wider, until I thought her eyeballs could quite possibly jump out of their sockets, in a springy-sprongy way. For there, high above the ground we had our feet so firmly earthed upon, passing to and fro on the balloon, was the bony outline of what passed for conversation between Momsie and Tom.

'That's unbelievabubble!' Granda wasn't thinking straight, for he definitely wasn't talking straight.

It took her a few moments longer but Siobhan soon found expression for her feelings, too. 'It's unballoonably amazing!' But then her face took on an angered red hue. 'Is that how the two of you knew so much about me and my friends? I don't believe it. You two were listening into, or watching into, my private conversations with my friends? Oh, to think . . .'

With that, Siobhan made for me, her arms flailing at the air between, nails on the out, ready, willing and wanting to skin me alive! I had to run, and quickly, as quickly as I could, because before I could do so, I had to pass the balloon cord over to Granda, and head straight through the nearest hedge to escape.

'When I get my hands on you, I'm going to . . . I'm going to take my revenge on your softest, sorest spots. You'll be lucky if you're still alive by the time I'm finished with you. In fact, you'll wish you were dead, really dead!'

Round and round the front garden we went, through hedges, over bushes, dodging branches, avoiding dead-ends, all the time keeping just enough space between us to keep me safe.

But I was soon feeling the pace, so the next time I circumnavigated the house, I back-looped in through the front door, squealed at Tom to 'Run for your life!' and headed straight upstairs and into the bathroom where

I bolted the door firmly shut before slouching down against it from sheer exhaustion.

Only a few restful minutes had passed, for me, anyway, when—

BOOM!!

I hesitated for a few moments by the window, but since neither of the other two showed in this time, I reckoned something horrible must have happened. I might not have been right but I knew I wouldn't be far wrong.

Out the bathroom door, across the landing, down the trouser-polished handrail as fast as the friction of my posteriored angle would allow for, I ran out of the house and straight into the disfigured face of Granda P. Then I caught sight of Siobhan and Tom, and they were beside themselves, as well as falling over each other, with paroxysms of mirth.

'I just . . . I just touched it, once, only once, and the bloody thing exploded in my face! Look at me, I'm scarred for life!'

Poor Granda. I tried to contain my laughter, I tried to hold it in, I tried to keep it at bay, but it wasn't very long before I, too, was roaring and snorting and squealing with delight.

'I'll be busy all day trying to peel this goo off my face. I don't suppose that father of yours has invented a gunk that will take this off my face while leaving my skin intact? No. It's more likely he thinks he has, but what he's come up with will take paint off walls instead. I'm away off to get cleaned!' And with that, a very sticky, masked

Granda P left the company of his three grandiosely giggling grandchildren.

By now we were unable to stand upright because of the level of hilarity coming out of every part of our beings and we were unable to advise Granda P whether hot or cold water would work best at taking it off. For all we knew, he might be best served by putting his head in a freezer for as long as it took for the gummy gum to harden and flake off. This was Siobhan's suggestion, transmitted just when we thought our three brains had managed to reconnect themselves to the giggling gangles of glee that had again taken possession of the three geeks within our skins.

It took us a long time to escape the enjoys of so much fun and it was only the sight of Granda P exiting the front door and heading over towards us that brought the three of us very quickly to our senses. We had to be very serious even though we couldn't help but wonder if Granda P had picked and washed the gum off his face with the aid of beetroot from a jar, so ruddy were his cheeks and chin.

'Come on, if we work hard we'll have this engine all set up and going by teatime. We can take it out on a test run then when we go for a bite to eat.' By now Granda P was right over beside us, and in a little aside he added, 'My favourite restaurant isn't so far from here, and it serves the most delicious cod and chips.'

We didn't need any more encouragement than that. If truth be told, we didn't need any encouragement at all. It was more than enough for us to believe ourselves to be valued members of a team involved in practical, worthwhile work. And so we got stuck into it. And so we did everything asked of us. And so we worked, sometimes above, sometimes underneath, the engine, pushing and shoving as best we could, holding bits and bobs in place while Granda P screwed and tightened.

And so the hours passed. And so we didn't notice darkness taking hold outside, for we were already working under light. And so when Granda P announced, 'That's enough for today, let's go and eat,' we downed tools immediately, stretched off the strains of physical work the like of which we had never before endured at Granda's, and smiled smile upon smile upon smile.

We stood proud in ourselves: proud of what we had done; proud of the blackness of our hands, our faces, even our clothes. The shrill shrieks and cries Momsie would undoubtedly have added to our sense of occasion were lost to our immediate sense of hearing but not to the inner attention of our understanding, the inner voice that still could be heard. For that's the way with mums; even when they're not there, you can still hear what they're saying.

'Jeepers, has anyone noticed the time?' Tom had only just claimed his watch back from its safe storage on top of an old dresser. 'It's nearly ten o'clock!'

Before any of the rest of us could manage to angle an eye in the direction of a wrist where a watch should be, Tom had answered his own question, and was now in the middle of opening the barn door to let a night-time of darkness in on us.

Amazing! We were totally stomped by this. And it was only then that stomachs began the intestinal chorus of calls encouraging us to find food and quickly shovel it down and into the rumbles of their desire.

'Ten o'clock, you say . . .' Granda didn't know whether to concentrate on scratching or shaking his head. 'Well, there's no point in a feed of fish and chips at this time of night, even if there was somewhere still open. Welsh rarebit all round – my treat – with a bottle of milk each. And we'll still have the restaurant to look forward to tomorrow.'

Smiles on the outside masked a feeling of deflation on the inside, although we couldn't help but agree with Granda's assertion.

So, while the three of us propped each tired and exhausted other up at the sink, scrubbing like mad with the nail brush when it finally came our turn to use it, Granda P got on with Welsh rarebiting toast and cheese together under the grill.

It was a veritable feast of plain eating and enjoyment, and we all went to bed happy, contented, and beside ourselves with sleep.

17 ZOOM-ZANG-ALANG!

Next morning we woke up – but only just. At almost midday we just about managed to crawl out of bed. By the time we made it through all the yawns and the slowest paces ever seen walking, while still managing to maintain a forward momentum, it was well into the first hour of the afternoon by the time we slid down to the bottom of the stairs.

Fortunately for us, Granda P was well into all that needed doing, and although we immediately got stuck into doing whatever he needed done, our pace was slow and it didn't seem to shift up a gear as the day moved nicely along. Thankfully for us, there wasn't too much that wasn't beyond near completion and soon enough, Granda P reckoned we were very nearly finished. So, it was not too long after that he poured a taste of petrol from a can into the engine and told us to stand well back because he was going to fire her up.

Well, what a buzz! It was brilliant! Our excitement was enormous, palpable, and although we mightn't have been able to touch it, we were certainly able to taste it.

The three of us stood, absolutely pulsating with anticipation, slightly worried in case it wouldn't happen, yet encouraged by our recent knowledge of a Granda P who had done so much, achieved so much, in life. This, therefore, would be a piece of cake to him. This business of attaching an engine to a car, a campervelle, and starting it up, was small fry to a magnificence of our granda's standing.

Ker – eh – heer – eh – heer – eh – heer – eh – heer – eh – heer – eh – heer – eh – hee.

A little line of worry suddenly appeared on Granda's brow.

Ker – eh – heer – eh – heer – eh – heer – eh – heer – eh – heer – eh – heer – eh – hee.

It was a nice sound. We were quite happy to hear any sort of a mechanical noise emanating from the internals of this beast of a machine. It's just that we knew it didn't lead onto the explosion of noise and metal, of chewing and rasping and rubbing together, cushioned by the soothiness of all that oil. It wasn't a mechanical orchestra warming up until it hit the right note that started it off and into a stronger and stronger line of power, more ebullient in terms of its internal humours, until it was formed and focused and bubbling over with the need to convert masses of power into energy to spin wheels and take off with the long, pent-up screeching of tyres.

Unfortunately, it was just the lonely rasping tune of a battery pulsating power into a unit that could not pick it up, and whose metal remained cold to the touch.

Ker – eh – heer – eh – heer – eh – heer – eh – heer – eh – heer – eh – heer – eh – hee.

Granda P offered it one last splurge of power from the battery, courtesy of his finger and thumb turning the ignition key, before he had to stand back and indulge in a good scratch of his cranium. Defeat stared him in the face. He didn't appear to have an answer to solve this one.

'Granda . . .' Siobhan stepped forward.

'Ssssshh! He's thinking!' I made a grab for her but Siobhan had no difficulty in pulling away from my pathetic attempt at stopping her. She then climbed into the wagen, and gently eased out a lever under the dashboard.

'Try it now, Granda.'

Granda leant in again and turned the ignition key. Unbelievably, like magic, the sweetest roaring blend of mechanical music started up inside the internals of the engine.

Granda's face lit up with it and immediately he threw himself round the back of the vehicle and got stuck into the engine with a long screwdriver, fine-tuning to a knowledge that was only in his hear. After another few minutes of ducking his head this way and that inside the engine bay, and pulling himself out of it every so often for a listen, the job was done. We were ready for take-off!

'You see, boys, that's what it's like to have a brain, to know what you're doing.' As he spoke, Granda P drew Siobhan into a great big bear hug with him.

Tom and my incommunicado self just stood there, feeling a bit left out, feeling more than just a little miffed. We weren't used to being beaten in macho matters like this by a girl – and certainly not by our sis.

'Watch you don't choke on your pride, boys.' Siobhan was ecstatic and she gave us both a double poke in the eye by way of the strongest of digs with her words.

We couldn't help but smile back at the pun of her display. We couldn't help but feel annoyed at ourselves for our total lack of thought here. Of course, a cold engine needs the choke in use to start it up! Why hadn't I thought of that? Internally, at least, Tom and my jealous self had to take our hats off to Siobhan; she had beaten us hands down on this one. We'd have to keep a close eye on sis from now on; she was a lot smarter than she gave herself credit for.

'Right, as soon as we're ready, it's off to town to fill up the tank with petrol. And to fill up our own tanks with something a lot tastier.'

Well, Tom and my expectant self seemed to have been standing in the hallway an endless age before Granda P honoured us with his presence, but it was well worth the wait. I had never before seen him look so majestic, so smart, so clean shaven, and smelling as though he hadn't held back in splashing half a bottle of the old love oil on his face. He was in the bubbliest form I had ever seen him in, all smiles and chit-chat and checking himself over more times than enough in the mirror than would normally have done him for a whole year.

And then we waited, and waited, and waited, but this

waiting didn't really matter, because Granda P was chin-wagging away, talking of this and that and the other, and then Siobhan made her royal entry. For the life of me, I couldn't see what had taken her so long, unless fashioning a scarf around her neck in the correct manner, in as much as there is a correct manner to do anything, could have taken her this length of time. Well, I suppose it was a very long scarf!

'Ah, I see you're wearing the scarf I bought your granny just before she left.' As an aside to Tom and my grinning self, Granda P added, 'She didn't follow my advice on how best to wear a scarf like that.' And with that, Granda P gave a pretend yonk on his cravat. 'You look absolutely beautiful with it on, which is more than I could ever honestly say about the original recipient of the gift!'

Piously smiling back at his own thoughts, Granda P led us out of the house, with Siobhan linked onto his arm as the lady of the moment, if not the lady of the house. The two of them swept out through the front door, across the applauding, appreciative gravel, and into the waiting magnificence of bright orange hue, while Tom and my cheerful self set ourselves up in the rear.

Zoom-Zang-Alang! Zoom-Zang-Alang! Zoom-Zang-Alang! Zoom-Zang-Alang! Zoom-Zang-Alang!

Our campervelle didn't miss a beat as it powered along the windy, bendy, narrow country road toward town. We were cock-a-hoop with the delight of it all. Perfectly balanced it was – Granda P had certainly done a pretty fine job with the suspension – and as for acceleration, well, it took off like a bullet along straight stretches of road and shot out of corners without the least constrain.

The only problem I had was in my head, and it was a dilemma Tom probably shared with me because it was something we had worked at together. How long was a gallon container of petrol going to last, especially driving like this?

Together we had painstakingly poured every last drop of this volatile liquid into the opening for the tank, taking particular care not to spill a drop on the unblemished paintwork. Granda was well away from us while we performed this exacting duty, supposedly attending to another job, but I knew he had an eye to what we were doing; we both knew this. But Granda P was learning that he didn't need to worry about us on that score, for meticulous was our measure in most of our deeds.

Soon enough, though, our breathing took on a more regular form when we caught sight of the local filling station. While Granda P got out and opened up the petrol cap for the dirty overalled young attendant who sauntered over at a pace all his own, the three of us sat in quiet but proud display of ourselves inside our magnificent orange horseless carriage.

Probably without thinking, the young lad landed a couple of hard pokes of his work boot on one of the tyres, when a bellowing voice caught him from behind and made his whole person jump in one involuntary action, before he hurriedly relieved Granda P of his petrol pumping duty. It was only then this assistant caught sight of something, or someone, more in line with his narrow range of interests, who was sitting imperiously in the front passenger seat.

The voice that had shaken this young apprentice from his first reverie, was now over talking with Granda, and it was obvious from the smiles and laughs of them that an old friendship was somewhere in the midst of their banter and jokes. And then the serious side of their two faces paced round the wagen, examining and inspecting, and giving many of the finer details the once over.

Before the attendant was finished his pumping duties – and it did seem to take him an inordinately long time to fill the tank – the boot lid was popped open and Granda P proceeded to rave about his new engine, almost as much as he railed against the original unit the poor beast had been lumbered with.

It was good to listen to this. It was somehow reassuring to hear two men, well on in terms of the years their ages added up to, rattling on at each other in the same way Tom and my brotherly self did, or like any two schoolboys did, except for the fact that what was being discussed passed for "grown-up" talk. Even then, when the engine lid was secured closed, they were still going on at each other with details of timings and settings and changes that should or shouldn't be made.

Meanwhile, the young pump-master extraordinaire obviously saw his opportunity and seized it with both dirty mitts, when he darted straight over to Siobhan's side window. On account of the good warmth that was in the day, she had the window right down, and she quickly had to slide herself over on her seat when the suspect being inside dirty overalls decided to shove his head, plus a good length of his upper torso, through the opening, uninvited of course.

'So, what are you doing tonight?'

As brazen as you like – he doesn't know her from Eve and he's already asking our sis out! Well, it didn't take any sort of a mind genius, like Tom or my hotshot self, to work out what was going on here.

'I'm going on a hot date with my fiancé! Why? Are you afraid to get into the bath on your own because you've lost your little duck?' And with this, Siobhan pushed her clean but cheeky face right up against his reddening features.

The poor cretin was more than just a little fazed by this. His shame was there for all to see on his scarlet pimpled countenance, freshly flushed with the humiliation of Siobhan's sharp tongue, as well as his own obvious stupidity.

By now the hapless attendant had recoiled a few paces, but there was no way out for him, he had no chance of an honourable retreat. In a vain and empty attempt at retrieving some dignity from an impossible situation, in other words making a bad situation worse, the pitiable fool had another go at making himself out to be more of an eejit than he already was.

'I wouldn't be seen dead in an old wreck like that. It's just a rust bucket tarted up!'

'I don't think there's any chance of that ever happening, unless Granda P decides to go into the undertaking business!' Tom delivered his epithet with all the gusto of an experienced Shakespearean actor.

Three silly big smiles staring his way, three bendy hands waving in his direction, meant he had no alternative but to turn away in a huff and take his temper out on a near perfectly rounded piece of gravel that had teed itself up nicely for the swipe of his big toe.

Thwack! Off the lovely little lump of gravel shot at a tremendous speed. And it didn't stop until it was well through the front window of the filling station shop.

SMACK! BANG! CRACK!

'Spud, you horrible little runt of a moron! You'll be working late every night for the next two weeks to pay for that! Get back in under a car where you belong!' Granda's old pal was now trying to get close enough to his numbskull employee to land his size ten upon the occasion of his posterior.

By now, too, Granda P had paid his petrol dues and was installed again behind the steering wheel of the campervelle. 'At the rate that old cudgel pays, the poor sod will be working overtime for the next two months to pay for his damage.'

A hollow feeling of *serves him right* ran through me, although Tom and my unspecified self did have to concur noddingly with Siobhan when she determined, 'Well, hopefully he'll learn a good lesson from this.'

Zoom-Zang-Alang! Zoom-Zang-Alang! Zoom-Zang-Alang! Zoom-Zang-Alang! Zoom-Zang-Alang!

To the smiles of some, the waves of many, and the consternation of one in particular, Granda P sped us across the forecourt and out onto the main road.

'Okay, kiddos, is there anything else we have to do before heading home?' The answer was already in Granda's tone as well as his look.

'Eat!!!' our trio of voices chorused from all around.

And that's exactly where we headed next – Fiorentini's Traditional Fish and Chip Shop, for nothing too fancy, nothing more than good ordinary food properly cooked. As far as their name went, they were certainly of Italian extraction, but according to Granda, it was well over a century since the last of their number had departed beautiful, sunny Italy for our dreary shores.

As we sat chatting, laughing, appreciating the enjoyment in satisfaction of it all, as we picked and flicked through the last of the dead-ends on our plates, Granda P said that magical word:

'Dessert!'

There was no question of what we were going to have. It was Knickerbocker Glories all round; well, for the three of us. Granda opted for a basic wafer configuration.

There is no possible way on this earth that any young, impressionable person worth his or her salt can resist such a boastful, ostentatious and brilliant a title as Knickerbocker Glory, filled as it is with more than just jocular hyperbole. Well, what a sight for sore eyes was the procession that brought the three Glories down into our midst, and it seemed more than slightly religious in connotation. And when we dipped the elongated shafts of our spoons into the absolute divinity of their creation, there was definitely no doubt about it in our minds: we were in heaven.

All this time, Granda P sat, perhaps the happiest of all, enjoying the togetherness of this family moment in a way that was more than evident in his eyes. And the ice cream wafer in his hand turned round and round and round as his tongue expertly shaved off the ample amount so tenderly pressed out by his thick-set fingers. Still, he had time to top off the moment with a disconcertingly small cup of frothy coffee, a cappuccino, which he offered around the screw-up of our faces, although the sprinkling of powdered chocolate on top was quite alluring.

'Oh, Granda, that's a horrid smell! How can you drink it?' Tom spoke for the three of us. At home, thankfully, Momsie and Dad were far from fans of the drinking habit that allowed this pungent aroma to distress our sense of smell.

'Ah, the smell's not too bad, but the taste is tremendous. A king to anything you might stir at home.' With his chin rising and his eyes closing, Granda P drank in the sweet scent curling up above his tiny cup. 'This is sheer bliss, absolute heaven!'

The problem for most people with being in heaven is that they think this is as good as it gets and they make do with it. Not with Granda P: he knew the way to super-heaven, and right then it was across the street and a few doors down!

It was the most expensive, and undoubtedly finest, chocolatier in this part of the country. It was the sort of shop we could never have bought in because even if we pooled all our money only then might we have had enough for one tiny but tasty creation. Today was different, though.

'Every vehicle should have a selection of the most yummy-yummily toothsome of sweet edibles to enhance the sense of occasion of every journey. Don't you agree?'

Who was this Granda-guy? He couldn't possibly be related to Momsie, could he? Doubts were beginning to grow in our minds!

Never before had we been witness to notes being passed over a counter for the purchase of sweets and chocolate. Terribly expensive sweets and chocolate they most definitely were, especially to young minds that only knew the rattle of small change when investing in the torture of our teeth.

Then, when we stepped out of the most expensive sweet shop in the whole world, decorative bag firmly clutched in Siobhan's hand, our day just kept going beyond better and better.

'Right, where are we off to now?'

All we could do was stare up at Granda; we didn't dare try to answer him in case what we came up with wasn't as good an idea as what he could come up with. He seemed a dab hand at this enjoyment business up to now.

'Well, I'm going to buy a newspaper; why don't you come along and select a magazine of your choice?'

Something inside my head told me, and probably registered inside the mind of each one of the three of us, that if we were with Granda P every day for a whole year, he'd probably act in the exact same way as he did today, every day – it was just his nature.

With our magazines selected and bag of swanky sweets at the ready, we headed for home. What a day we were having, and it was still nowhere near teatime, yet!

We took the scenic route back, along which Granda P could survey the sites he wanted to see, as well as pass a few places of work, worship, and whatever, where he could toot the horn – worked by dabs of the fingers rather than a firm push of the hand – and we were all lost for words for a while.

The main reason for the sibling silence was the deliciousness of sweetnesses being passed around by Siobhan from the bag she had control over, which meant our inner senses were completely taken over by new and thrilling taste sensations. Therefore, for a short time, only Granda P had control of his power of speech.

And so, a dozy quality took hold of the three of us as we settled back into thoughts of our own make and manage, and barely a word was uttered by any one of us on the travel homewards because not a word needed said.

18 SPLASHY PURSUIT

'Aha! What's all this, then?'

I don't know if it's possible to imagine the startle that ran through us, that made us jump inside our skins, and frightened us back into life. Granda P had transported us almost to our destination when he had pulled up suddenly and almost whispered his almost question.

Across in the distance, we could see Gooseberry House, and all seemed normal around it, except for a white van that was parked outside the front door.

Three men – and it didn't take a genius to work out who these three were – were carrying out a television and other electricals from Granda's house and loading them into the back of their van! Siobhan, Tom and my stumped self were too stunned to know what to say, perhaps too scared within ourselves to be able to speak.

'This requires a bit more investigation. Let's watch and see what happens next.' Granda sounded so calm and controlled, as if he was well used to situations like this.

I don't think it was by chance that Granda P had parked the orangeness of our means of transportation behind the cover of a good thick hawthorn hedge along the side of the road, but at an angle that afforded us a good view of proceedings.

'Well, we know who they are, and we can see what they're up to. Let's take our time and see where they go from here.'

There was measure in Granda's voice. There was a drift running through his tone that he was no stranger to this watching and waiting game. Time was indeed the only thing that would let us into what would happen next and we had it in plentiful supply.

Waiting isn't all it's drummed up to be because, first of all, you need to have plenty of patience, and, secondly, you need to have even more patience. I had some patience and my some amounted to a little more than Siobhan's and a little less than Tom's. Therefore, while sis fidgeted and futtered with anything and everything she could lay her hands on, Tom and my spying self kept an eye on the thieving business happening at the house, and a closer eye on what was unravelling in the stories in our magazines. This way, it didn't seem to take as long for the white van men to finish their wrongful doings and head off.

Strangely, they didn't head back our way, but, instead, took a right-handed turn at the bottom of Granda's long, treed driveway, as if they were heading for the beach. In fact, they had to be heading for the beach because there was nowhere else they could go.

'I wonder what they're up to now?' Granda P gave voice to the question tumbling about in three younger heads.

We knew it wouldn't take long to find out because the robbers were making haste toward a dead end. The only road hereabouts was the one they were presently scurrying along, which meant at some point they would have to do an about-turn and find a way past us if they were to escape. So, Granda P took his time, driving very slowly, obviously in no hurry to catch up with them. Well, it wasn't as if they had anywhere else to go. But they did.

'Stop, Granda! They've cut off to the right!' Fortunately for us, Tom noticed fresh tyre tracks on the rutted, muddied entrance to a field close by the beach. I don't know about Siobhan, but I wasn't able to speak because my heart was in my mouth.

Granda braked quickly and we were just in time to catch the end of the white van as it ploughed its way off the field and onto the scraggy bit of ground between it and the beach.

'The tide will be on the turn soon, so they'll need to be quick about what they're doing. Interesting guys, these; I'm beginning to think we shouldn't underestimate them. Their recklessness is in what they do, not in the way they do it.'

Granda was right. These thieves had obviously preplanned everything they were at, because if they hadn't, they were going to be in a right nasty pickle with an immeasurable amount of salty water lapping up their legs.

'What are they playing at? Driving down the back part of Paddlers' Beach, when along there there's nothing but cliff face . . . and Smugglers' Cave! Of course, why didn't I think of it before? There's even a natural, raised part inside where they can store their loot, maybe even park their van!' Granda thumped the steering wheel with his clenched fist; fortunately for us, it was nowhere near the centre of it.

'They wouldn't be able to store it in there for very long; the saltiness of the seawater is bound to play havoc with any electric or electronic goods they've stolen.' Siobhan really was operating in intelligent mode today.

Then, just as Granda P had suspected, the van turned out toward the waves before reversing into what must have been Smugglers' Cave, but we couldn't say for sure from our vantage point. All we could see was that it seemed to disappear into the coastline.

'What do we do now?'

As soon as I said it, I knew I should not have bothered opening my mouth because all I was doing was asking what was already glaringly obvious. There was only one reply to this and it came jointly from all the others:

'Wait!!!'

I've always found that no matter how little time you actually spend doing it, when you have to wait, it works against your whole personality. It never failed to leave me feeling anything other than every minute took an hour in real time to pass. And now was certainly no different. So, after about a whole day spent inside ten minutes tennissing the idea to and fro inside my head, I slid open my side door and descended from the campervelle.

'I need to pee.'

I didn't really, but I thought I might as well, there being nothing else of note either happening or about to happen and my words having evoked not even a murmur of a response from any of the others. I was less than halfway through when I heard the enormous roar of an engine nearby.

'Get in quickly!' was the sudden order that panicked me.

I've started, so I'll finish! was the only line that came into my head in response, but I was too busy trying to deal with my undoing to distract myself any more than I didn't need to.

At least I could be excused not seeing a large boat being dragged down to the water. I don't know what the rest of them must have been doing, daydreaming, or reading, or fantasising about becoming Spiderman or Superwoman, or Superman or Spiderwoman.

Whatever the way of it, their eyes were off what they should have been on. Whatever Granda's great hurry was, he had the wagen in gear and was hurtling headlong toward the briny blue beyond before I had myself fully reinstalled inside, not to mention having the door only half closed. Yes, that's right, he was heading straight for the washy waves of the sea!

It was beginning to look like Granda P had taken leave of his senses because, instead of swinging the steering wheel around and avoiding contact with the salty water, he flicked and clicked at switches on the dash. In one long wail of a sound, the trio of voices around him cried:

'Grandaaa!!!'

However, there wasn't time to jump overboard or go searching under seats to see if there were any life jackets safely stashed. We were in splashy pursuit – and there was no turning back.

'Don't worry, kiddos, I've built her for every eventuality . . . I hope.'

It was his last two words that I didn't like the sound of, which filled me with dread and the want to avoid a watery grave. Granda, too, seemed to add a bit more thought to what he had said, and his afterthought made me go all weak at the knees.

'*Almost* every eventuality!'

Serious gulps of worry held the strangle of our throats, and we edged frightened bodies away from doors we sat against, as all young eyes became glued to the bottom joins of these, expecting at least a trickle of seawater to be finding its way in by now.

'Will she float?'

At any other time, Siobhan's question might have sounded silly; right now, it seemed the most salient question in the whole world. It was the one question that needed asking. Even more to the point, though, it was the one that needed answering.

'We'll soon find out. Ready, everyone. Here goes!'

With that, we could hear the wash of watery waves all around, but it wasn't quite possible yet to feel whether we were floating, or sinking.

'I've an aluminium base on her, completely sealed, engine bay double sealed. Exhaust fumes are piped up and out the metal cap on top at the rear. We're propelled by the number plates, front and rear; highly experimental so I'm not quite sure about the settings yet. I'm beginning to think I should have added a little more angle to the twist.'

Granda sounded reasonably confident. Anyway, he wouldn't have driven us into a soaky end, would he? I said nothing. We all said nothing, because there was nothing to say. It was too late for words! Now, all that could save us was Granda's expertise.

My eyes flicked back and forth with the monotonous drive of the windscreen wipers. My mind flicked from a mechanical obsession with these and down into a blind state of panic as I microscoped around for trickles or dribbles, or worse, of salty water. To my immense relief, there didn't appear to be even a droplet anywhere, and by now I was searching all over, scanning in behind as well as alongside.

'How's she looking? Is everything watertight?'

I caught the look of Granda's eyes off the rear-view mirror as he asked. I don't know whether he expected a response in the negative, but I could tell he didn't want one; either way, he didn't get one.

'All clear and dry so far.' This was the general consensus.

'I think she's pulling a bit to the right – sorry, starboard, I should say. I'll have to allow for that in my steering.' Granda sounded as if he might be deriving some enjoyment from this. He certainly didn't appear in the least put out by any of it.

'Granda . . .'

Tom and my inquiring self both stared over at Siobhan, mainly because of the little-girl-lost voice she had used. It was always interesting to us to hear what would follow on from this.

'We don't appear to be going very fast, certainly not in comparison to the robbers' speedboat.'

It was a leading statement of fact, but where it was leading was a bit like ourselves heading out to sea: we didn't know yet but we had a feeling we would soon find out.

'Well, perhaps you could ask them to slow down for us?' Granda P took a sideways swipe with his look at Siobhan and drew in a deep breath. 'It's her maiden voyage . . .'

I think the truth of what we were at, what we were doing, had just begun to dawn on Granda, and he would only have been showing signs of being normal to be worried, very worried. However, the depth of the silence that came after told him this wouldn't do.

'I built this for pleasure cruising, not for pounding the high seas. I don't know how well she's going to cope with the waves out in the middle of the vast blue briny.' Tension was palpable in Granda's tone.

This was more than enough to send our minds into recoil, to halt our heroic hankering of becoming hunters of the high seas. In my mind, this was all very well for Siobhan and Tom; they both had gained their life-saving medals from the swimming club back home. I, on the other hand, had cheated with my feet when I swore I swam a whole width of the four-foot deep section of the pool. It must be true, then – lying to your mum will always come back and haunt you!

'In theory she'll be fine. And there's no problem with theory until it rewrites itself, usually by something going wrong. I'll give it a go, though.'

Granda looked worried, but he piled on the power and we could feel a great surge catch our beast of a machine and push her along with increased energy, increased enthusiasm, through the wash of the waves. However, the further out from dry land we went, the choppier the sea became, and the worse we were all feeling inside our well-stuffed stomachs.

'Oh, I can feel that Knickerbocker Glory splashing about inside me!'

I knew what Tom was up to and I decided to join him.

'Oh, I can feel all the fish and chips being battered about inside me. In fact, I wouldn't be too surprised if they popped up for another visit!'

I then made a few barfy noises and a few bokey sounds. The change in alignment of Granda's wrinkles showed he knew exactly what we were at, but then he knotted an eyebrow into his look in the mirror just for us.

'Stop it, you two. You know I don't like being in a boat, on the sea, with the waves crashing about us, up and down, up and down . . .' Siobhan didn't sound at all well, but her cheeks still had plenty of colour in them, and she kept a firm grip of the door handle, which obviously helped maintain enough of her equilibrium.

If the main reason for our episode of comedic

endeavour had been to blanket our inner fear from our outer selves, it worked, but only for a matter of minutes. Then, the reality of our situation was right there in our focus, and something stirring in the pit of my stomach suggested this wasn't the greatest idea ever. And what's more, we were no longer playing catch-up with the three thieves who were disappearing into the distance. And even more than what's more, the sea was getting rougher and starting to take command of our misshapen vessel instead of vice-versa.

'I think we need to change course. Is everyone agreed?'

I knew Granda P was trying to sound as upbeat as possible – we all did – but it wasn't working very well. He looked right round the rise and fall of three nodding heads that might well have been nodding simply because of our course through the waves.

'Okay. Hold onto whatever you can, because this has never been tried before! Certainly not on the high seas, and definitely not in this colour of a campervelle!'

19 FLYING HIGH

With the crashing waves threatening to drag us under, Granda P threw caution to the seas and took command. He gave a good, hard thump on the horn, followed by a continued and pressurised push. Immediately, and thankfully, the mechanism above our heads in the middle of the wagen began unravelling itself, unfolding its rubbery texture out and upwards.

'Balloon up?'

In the silence that followed came the realisation that Granda P was voicing a deliberately loud checklist of what he was doing off against his mental checklist of what needed to be done.

'Balloon up!' Together, Tom and my militaristic self reiterated what Granda P needed to hear.

'Right, what's next?' Granda said this in a way that obviously meant he was asking it of himself, not of the rest of us. Fortunately, he remembered straight away.

'Helium on?' The push of his forefinger into an awkwardly positioned afterthought of a button brought out the sound of hissing on either side of Tom and my bemused self, as well as above our heads. The immediate aftermath of this was like a feeling of lightness being brought to bear on the campervelle, as the thump of sea waves on her structure lessened with our rise up out of the enormity of water that was acting as if it wanted to swallow us up.

'Helium on!!' We reiterated what was said.

Then Granda P flicked another switch, this time one above his Blaupunkt radio unit. 'Propeller on forward thrust.'

From where I was seated I could just about see it. The large VW badge at the front of the wagen sprung out and unfolded itself in the same movement; then it started spinning, quick, quicker, quicker, until it had itself powered up to a rate of spins whereby it was impossible to see anything but a haze around the end of its extended arm.

'Front propeller on forward thrust.' This duty befell Siobhan, and she spun her words out with aeronautical precision. Granda gave a sideways glance at sis and smiled brilliantly.

Not only were we now rising quickly through the above with great upwards momentum, but our whole contraption seemed wonderfully suited to its new found role, flying expeditiously through the air. I was glad to be up and out of the water – I think we all were – for the wagen seemed totally unsuited to its battle through the waves. Now we were powering along nicely – so well, in fact, that we again caught sight of the robbers' fast motorboat, away off in the distance. A distant thought then seemed to wander slowly into my mind.

'Granda . . .' – I caught his backwards look in the mirror – 'how will you know when you've enough helium pumped into the balloon?'

'That's easy, you'll tell me.' The wrinkles from his smile showed up on every part of his face that I could see in the mirror.

'What?' I didn't know how I was meant to tell Granda P something I didn't know, and, perhaps more relevantly, had no way of telling. The shrug of Tom's shoulders when I looked questioningly over at him showed he was as much in the dark about it as I was.

Siobhan, of course, smiled graciously up at Granda P in the subliminal way girls have of showing they understand something, whether or not they actually do. Granda smiled knowingly back at his granddaughter and then angled his head round toward Tom and my stupefied self.

'You'll find it funny.'

Either Granda P had started to lose his marbles with the deoxygenation of the air as we went higher and higher up, or Tom and my blank self had missed something. And something important, too. I have to admit, I thought the latter of these two suggestions to be the most probable. And this was verified seconds later when I began to laugh, as did Tom, probably at the absurdity of what Granda P had said, although I was very far from being sure about this or anything else for that matter.

What started off as a light piece of laughter between the two of us soon became a serious fit of eye-watering, snotter-inducing, rib-tickling, side-splitting frenzy of farcical delirium, especially when Granda P said to Siobhan, 'Helium off?' The way he said it was so funny.

And when she responded with, 'Helium off,' she sounded like a squeaky robot, and what had been hilariously funny moments before now became hysterically farcical. I was sure a permanent dysfunction of my brain would happen with so much uncontrollable laughter. Tom and my silly self were about to slide under our seatbelts and off our seats with the volcanic eruption of imbecility that had taken control of a very determined corner of our inner selves.

Then I caught the look on Granda's face as he stared over at Siobhan after hearing her high-pitched voice, having only just latched onto the way he himself had spoken. 'I think I might have used too much!' he squeaked.

Hearing a squeegee, Donald Duck-like voice, emanate from the ultra-mannish frame of Granda P was the funniest thing I had ever heard, the funniest thing I had ever seen, and left me in the funniest way I had ever been. By now, both Tom and my uncontrollable self were on our knees on the back floor, hardly able to see, so runnily were tears dripping from our eyes.

'Eh, what's up, Doc?'

Tom's voice was mayhem personified, and by now we were unable to see anything but the underside of the seats we should have been sitting on. And so it continued, our sharp, shrill sounds being added to by the driver and front-seat passenger, although they did manage to retain a semblance of respectability about themselves, as well as some sort of control over our mode of travel.

Normality took its time returning to the inner contain, the outer aspect, of our persons, but eventually we did manage to reposition our posteriors onto the hold of our seats, and not before time, too. And just in time for our minds to capture the truth of what was happening to us. We were flying!

'This is splendacular!'

'It's terrificent!'

'Dazzalistic!'

'Superbulous!'

'Fantashing!'

'Awesomnable!'

'Phenomulous!'

'Magnifastic!'

'Wonderendous!'

'I'm just glad it works so well. Now let's see where they've gotten to.'

After smiling round the good-humoured measure of our fantastical words, Granda P humped his shoulders up, his head down, and his right shoe sank the accelerator pedal into the plush depth of carpet underfoot.

'They're well ahead of us but we can still see where they're going. We'll need to keep a closer eye on proceedings for it looks as if they're heading for the islands.' Granda was sounding normal again now, his squeakiness of voice having left him, having left us all; so it was a lot easier to think rationally again.

Sure enough, far off in the distance, the powerboat looked as if it was sure to crash into a rocky outcrop of land straight ahead of it. Then, unexpectedly, it took a sharp turn to go toward the second island, instead of avoiding it completely as it could have done. From our vantage point it looked like crazy driving, especially when it slammed down to a snail's pace, obviously closing in on its target area, as it crawled around its jagged southern edge before heading straight ahead.

From our angle, it was impossible to ascertain exactly what happened the robbers' boat next. But we knew it had either crashed into the rocks and had immediately sunk, or it had gone straight into another cave. Although we hadn't seen for sure, we knew it must have entered another cavernous hideaway.

By now, though, the wind had picked up and Granda P was having difficulty manoeuvring our bulky weight. In fact, if truth be told, we were all feeling more than just a little bit nervous, because he was having difficulty keeping her at the angle of level and balance that we needed.

'The wind that so kindly helped carry us here has picked up and now wants us to continue our travels, just when we would rather land. We'll have to take her down quickly otherwise we'll be hard pressed to re-find this point of their disappearance.'

Granda had assumed a stern look; he gritted his teeth and gave a good yonk on a handle above his door. Immediately, too immediately for my liking, we began to lose height.

My heart, and a few other necessaries of internal functioning not so firmly attached to where they belonged, saw their opportunity to escape and went for it. Fortunately, my teeth were awake to what was going on and they slammed firmly shut so all my internal bits and bobs had to settle back down to their belong.

I watched and braced myself as Granda's hand reached up for the handle again. Thankfully, this time it appeared to lessen our descent speed, but we were once again being tossed around dangerously by the wind.

'This is our maiden flight as well as our maiden voyage, so you'll have to forgive me if I'm a bit rusty in landing this machine. Well, not really rusty because . . .'

Here, as Granda's small talk stalled, the three of us smiled proudly over at this genius of a relation who could do anything – we hoped.

'Because I've never really landed it before!'

The only thought that came into my head was the oft-repeated one from home: *There's a first time for everything!* And I now hoped against hope that this was wrong, today at least. A terrible cringing feeling burst on three insides and hit the cover of three young faces who found it impossible to hide the look of fear.

'Oh, the theory's perfectly fine, based on my knowledge and rememberings of the workings of balloon flight. It's managing it all for the first time again that is the difficulty. Guiding the descent of such a heavy machine isn't as easy as I had imagined, and we're not getting much help from the strong wind.'

As his words finished, Granda P gave another pull on the handle, only this time it was a longer, more sustained pull, which didn't appear to be as hard or sharply initiated. It certainly had more of the desired effect than the first yonk of the handle had. I looked up and saw little flaps at the top of the balloon open to release the transparent gas that was keeping us airborne on our daring, high-flying mission chasing after the three robbers.

'If we ever get safely back down onto *terra firma*, I've had enough of this highfalutin business to last me a lifetime. I think I'm starting to get too old for all of this.'

There was obvious worry sounding through Granda's words, an uneasiness he duly passed onto the rest of us to make of what we would.

Our rate of descent was still too rapid and needed to ease off or else we were going to make a very large dent on the side of a grassy hill we were hurrying to a horrible halt on. It was definitely the island we were headed for. We weren't going to be saved by a stupendous splash on the surface of the salty sea. Something needed doing and in a mighty fine hurry!

'Okay, I think it's time for emergency action!'

Granda was looking at Siobhan as his words marched out with great gravitas and into the console of our listen. Siobhan smiled bravely back. Tom and my mollified self each eased out a sigh of relief. At least now we knew there was a chance of salvation, and it befell Siobhan to save us all.

'Open the glove compartment and pull the lever on the right.'

No sooner had Siobhan been told what to do than she had it done. And with a whoosh of wind and scramble of strings and urgency of unfurling, a gleaming white parachute affair sprang from its secret space in the canopy above. It billowed out in all its puffed up glory and, within moments, our rate of descent slowed to that of a veritable feather floating down to land. And when I looked out my side window, I saw several sheep, rather belatedly but wisely, scampering rapidly out of our way.

Then . . .

KERTHUMP!!

20 ISLAND ANTICS

'Hurrrraaayy!!!!'

Four throats added their presentation of sound to the still vibrating springs and sprongs of the wagen as it came to rest in a now-deserted field. For a few seconds, it was the nicest possible feeling on earth to be back on dry land. Until, one by one, our memories were jolted back into the remember of what we were doing here, and why we had travelled so far after the thieves.

Granda got out and had to stand on the side runs to refold and reposition the parachute back into its fixes in the canopy space.

'The emergency chute was a good idea after all. I'm glad I overcame my doubts and installed it.' Granda was talking away to himself while at the same time airing messages to us, making sure we were aware of exactly what was what in the grandafacture of our vehicle.

Soon, in an awkward effort of a way, the campervelle made its way down and off the field and onto the wonderful feel of a clean sweep of gravelly tarmacadam under its treads. It was a sharp right-hand turn toward the area of coast into where the robbers and their boat had disappeared.

'There aren't many living on the outer parts of the islands these days; even the lighthouse is on automatic. But the roads are still intact for the visitors that Summer brings.' Granda, as usual, had the know of our whereabouts.

At least this was something positive; it was good that we wouldn't have to do too much off-roading. I had noticed, during our more leisurely descent, there were still a good few cottages and houses scattered around and about, and any of the trees still standing were generally clustered around these; they must originally have been planted as some form of protection from the drive of winter wind and rain. However, it was plain and obvious to see many of the roofs of these dwellings had fallen in, long since unable to cope with the rigours of abandonment.

We hadn't been very long travelling down the loneliness of a deserted road when I thought I saw something unusual out of the corner of my eye. In fact, it wasn't an actual something that I saw, rather a something that didn't add up. A few moments later I caught it again, only this time I had been half on the lookout for it. By the time we had Zoom-Zang-Alanged for a good distance down the road, I was sure and certain of what I had seen and I was waiting for it to happen again.

'Stop! Stop the car! Stop the wagen!' Like an auto-reflex, the words self-activated from inside me.

Granda P pulled the campervelle up sharpish in the

middle of the single-track road we had been hurrying along.

'What? What is it?' Granda swung round in his seat as he asked. I think he thought something must have happened to me.

'Look . . .' I pointed out the window. 'It's a kind of camouflage someone has used on these houses. They look dilapidated and broken down from above, as well as from here, but it's all a disguise to conceal the fact that they're fully roofed.'

I didn't know if I was making myself totally clear. I sensed I wasn't. So, I continued on with what I had already begun to say. 'Can you see it? You must be able to see it. They must have used paint or . . .'

'Gosh, yes, look. That's amazing! It's really well done.' Now he could see it for himself, Tom believed me. He could see someone had gone to a lot of expense and bother in an effort to conceal the fact that this house was being used for something. If this was the case, it didn't take a genius to work out that whoever it was, was up to no good. Eventually, too, by leaning backwards instead of forwards, Siobhan and Granda P saw it.

'Well, we're in the right spot. There's certainly something untoward going on hereabouts!' Granda was undoubtedly correct, and the Zoom-Zang-Alang of the engine was once again taking us off in the direction of what we had fully determined inside our heads, as well as our hearts, to be trouble.

'We'll park here and shift the rest of the way on shank's mare, okay?'

There was no way we could or would disagree with something we didn't fully understand. So, an unsure trio echoed a shared 'Okay' back in Granda's direction. Then we all headed off on foot.

'Maybe we should head down to the coast first and then make our way round to the cave? It should be easier to find that way.' We hadn't been off on our cross-angled trek for very long when Tom decided to enlighten us with his good idea, by asking and answering in the one breath. However, it wasn't as well received as it was sent.

'That's what we're doing!'

It was obvious Granda P was feeling far from bowled over by what we were doing. It is probable he was worried for our safety; I know he would not have been worried for his own. The idea of us now getting close to the three robbers was bad enough, but there might well be a lot worse than them hereabouts, especially the likes of this French Henri character and his band of despicables.

There wasn't much of a banking down to the rockiness of the coastline, and we carefully clambered over these slippery surfaces until we noticed a large opening in the rock. We all recognised it as the spot the motorboat had last been seen heading towards from our previous airy vantage point.

That's when I looked round to see if any of the others could hear the pounding of my heart. And that's when I saw, in the strained look of everyone else there, that mine wasn't the only heart thumping hard and heavily, trying to tell me something I already knew as it battered against the insides of my ribcage. There was no hiding the look of fear and anticipation on every one of our faces. We didn't know what we were getting ourselves into, but we were determined to find out.

Granda was first to edge his way in, and Siobhan was right beside him, with Tom and my nervous self bringing up the rear. Thankfully, there was still plenty of light in the day to show us the way ahead; the sun might have been low in the sky but this proved perfectly suited to lighting up our careful passage in.

We moved stealthily, furtively dodging from rock to rock, with legs, bodies and heads ducked down, and every sense at our disposal placed on high alert lest we should be spotted and caught. Following along after Granda, making every move he made, avoiding every move he didn't make, obeying every silent command he gave, we made good progress.

It was like a military exercise, where Granda P signalled mainly with his hands but also with nods and nuances as well. Therefore, when Granda's eyes tightened and his nods quickened, we knew to blaze a trail as fast as we possibly could. When his lips pursed tightly and his brow lowered right down, we knew to go as quietly as possible, lest we be heard.

I didn't know where Granda P learned all his moves and manoeuvres but they were brilliant, because he was brilliant, and, once we got going, not for one moment did we feel overly worried about what we were at.

Then, at the end of the waterline, below where we were moving, at last we saw the robbers' motorboat. There was no point in going out of our way and tampering with it, and so we ignored it for the moment and kept on along the level we had journeyed this far.

As we moved further forward, the light began to fade, but not for very long. A different kind of light, artificial in its blend of colour, now fed out upon us from deep within the cave's interior. Now, as we moved forward, our hearts were pumping red alert into every particle of ourselves, for we sensed it wouldn't be long before we would be upon the three thieves we had followed, plus God alone knows who and whatever else.

As the strength of the light grew in our surrounds, we crouched our bodies down even further, for we knew now we had entered upon the lion's den. Then we heard voices. My heart tried to leap out of my mouth. This was real. This was now. And these were unmistakeably voices, but whatever way the words bounced off the craggy surrounds of the internals of the deep cave, it was near impossible to make out what was being said. In fact, it was far from clear what language they were speaking, shouting and guffawing in.

Granda sat us down around him. He didn't say a word. His message was loud and clear, though. Did we want to go back or did we want to push forward into the danger and uncertainty this undoubtedly brought with it?

There was no way we were backing out now. There was no way we would ever back away from a problem that needed dealing with. We weren't like that. We certainly weren't brought up like that. It was onward, forward, to see this through to the end. And so we pushed on, on our hands and knees now, and internally we steeled ourselves for what was to come.

Soon, we were in close enough, or as close as we wanted to be, which was definitely a lot closer than it was safe to be. We were tucked in behind Granda, who was behind a clump of rock that provided us with an excellent view. And here we watched.

As far as we could see, there were seven men below. Our three robbers had been joined by four others. I think they were French, for there were words said that certainly sounded French. It was more than obvious what was going on. The three thieves had brought over a boatload of stolen merchandise, mainly electrical and electronic, but also silverware such as candlesticks and cutlery, and jewellery – lots and lots of shiny, sparkling jewellery.

Behind the four foreigners there was a wooden case with its top wrenched off. Inside this there was the coldest display of guns I have ever seen: pistols, rifles, machine guns, plus whatever else lay underneath, for the wooden case was at least a foot in depth. There was no doubting what was happening: they were bartering – two sets of thieves trafficking by exchange their ill-gotten goods. This was certainly how it looked, how it sounded at first glance to me.

'Keep your heads well down. This doesn't look good. Those Frenchies have themselves positioned for action – military action!' Granda's whispers sent alarm bells ringing inside my head.

I don't know how bartering achieves its end when two different languages are involved. With the Frenchmen not seeming to have a word of English, and the

Englishmen trying their best in broken English and French and words that sounded as if they didn't belong in either language, not much progress was being made – quite the reverse in fact.

The three thieves were trying their damnedest to get their hands on the guns, probably to show how many pieces they wanted in exchange for the booty they had smuggled over. The Frenchies were having none of it, shouting and roaring, pointing and clicking their guns at them. And the more the three robbers tried to show what they wanted, the more resistant the Frenchmen were, even though they didn't budge from where they stood. All the air in the cave suddenly seemed full with tension and fear. Then there was mayhem.

When one of the thieves eventually did manage to get his hands on a gun, to show what he meant, a shot was fired – not quite *at* him, more *past* him – and this was followed by a few more shots being discharged. If this had happened outside, under the wrap of sky high above, it would have sounded bad enough. Happening inside a cave, the echoing sound of one shot reverberated as it bounced all around, sounding as if ten shots had been fired, with bullets seeming to ricochet everywhere.

Not only were the four of us as tightly ducked down as was possible, but we were squashed into the gather of one another so closely, we must have looked like another rock ourselves. It seemed like a long time later, although it was probably only seconds, when our necks began to rise up out of our bodies again and we peeped our eyes upon the expected scene of carnage below.

Shouts and roars in English as well as in French could be heard echoing all around, although there was not a single person to be seen. But at least now the sounds of bullets dancing and glancing, skipping and hitting off surfaces all about, had stopped.

'*Arrêtez! Arrêtez!* Stop! Stop!' were the distinguishable commands now holding sway over all other sounds therein.

By now the pandemonium had stopped, and as hands first appeared from behind clumps of rock, heads quickly followed. Then the leader of the French four went over to one of his number, hit him a good thick slap across the back of the head, and relieved him of possession of his gun.

'You fool! Are you trying to kill us all?'

The dunce who had just been dispossessed of his weapon stood with his head down, but he was obviously empty-headed enough to mutter something indistinct back in French. Another good hard slap quickly followed. What was easy to see from this one-sided discussion was that Monsieur Henri was definitely the one doing all the slapping and telling off, for he certainly wasn't one to accept dissent from amongst his own number.

The guns were immediately stashed back in their box and the lid firmly hammered down. Monsieur Henri then rounded on the three English, his arms open wide, gesticulating for them to come forward, not to be afraid, for they were his oldest and bestest friends in the whole wide world. Needless to say, the three robbers were scared and wary, and busy, too, staring at each other's reactions, but they were mighty relieved not to have been hurt.

With all the guns safely secured, and the leader of the French heading over toward the English in as friendly a manner as he could manage, a great feeling of relief entered upon the proceedings.

Monsieur Henri was hugging the English in the way the French do, but as he did so, he obliquely manoeuvred them round so they were facing out of the cave. Now, with all the chat and banter going on between them, the three thieves didn't notice what was going on behind their backs. While the really stupid one continued rubbing at the back of his head and muttering indistinct sounds to himself, his two compatriots were busy shifting another munitions box out from behind a rock and switching it with the one containing the guns.

'Take all the guns, put them in your boat now, so you can take them with you later – after we do the job we've planned!'

It was a miracle! A man who, minutes before, seemingly couldn't string two words of English together, now had perfect command of the thieves' vernacular.

I'm not sure whether the three English had lost their understanding of their own language, or had somehow lost the use of their voices. Whatever the way of it, they didn't say a word, and I don't think it was a sudden embarrassment of shyness that held them back. The truth, I'd say, is a lot closer to the fact that they were scared silly by what had happened and they didn't know what to expect next.

The white-van driver and boat steerer, the bearded Harry, eventually plucked up enough encouragement and re-found his voice, hoarsely at first, and frightened throughout its stuttering use.

'I . . . I . . . think we'd rather be heading back . . . across the water . . . if that's all right with you?' He had suddenly developed a severe nervous twitch as well, as he shared his hopes.

'Nonsense, nonsense, the job will go ahead and then you English go home and live happily ever after! Isn't that how you speak?'

By now also, the two Frenchies à la box had settled its heavy weight into the back of the motorboat. By now, too, the leader of the French, Monsieur Henri, had his arm around the bearded van driver and was leading him away, knowing his two accomplices would have to follow.

'Come on, come on, English. It's the easiest bank job in the whole world. The tunnel is dug, we're ready to break through, but we need you to open the safe. Simple as that! What could be easier? *N'est-ce pas?*'

Monsieur Henri continued talking as they disappeared up a set of old wooden stairs and around a corner where we couldn't see. As the rest of the would-be bank robbers followed wearily along behind, we watched as they, too, disappeared from sight. Then we heard what must have been a heavy metal door slam shut and locks being bolted.

Not a single, solitary word was uttered by any one of us, so lost were we in the unreality of what we had been witness to. We were trying to get to grips with the scariness of it all. Not to mention the knowledge we had of knowing we were going to have to do more – and it would probably be a lot more dangerous, too.

'Aaahh!'

A small screech rang out from Siobhan and echoed its way into every corner of the cave. We stared at her in horror, knowing the gang might not yet be away, and if this was the case they would definitely be able to hear a solitary sound like that rising up through the stillness and silence of the place, thus alerting them to our presence beneath.

Siobhan pointed at Granda, at his shoulder, the one I couldn't see because of the angle he was at. I looked at Tom, enquiring if he had any knowledge of what sis was on about. Tom puckered his eyebrows, furrowed his forehead and shrugged his shoulders. Then, as Granda P shifted round to face us, as he sought to see what the commotion was all about, we saw for ourselves. Blood! There was a big soak of blood that had stained its way down Granda's shirt.

'Granda, you've been shot!' As soon as she said this, Siobhan fainted, and it was all Tom and my acrobatic self could do to grab hold of her before she cracked her head on the rock we were still half hidden behind. Fortunately, she was only out of it for a matter of seconds, and was soon standing dreamily amongst us with the support of two brotherly arms, while our three sets of eyes stared unbelievably at the bloody mess on the sleeve of Granda's shirt.

By now, Granda P had himself well examined and was taking no notice of any of it. 'Come on, we'd better find our way out of here before they make their escape.' Granda winced a little as he made to make his move.

'Your arm, Granda . . . it's . . . you've . . .' The right words were in my head but they got stuck somewhere in the short distance between where the brain picks them up and the tongue rolls them out. Tom helped me here.

'Granda, you've been shot!' We stared over at the tear and bloody mess of his shirtsleeve, and wondered at what damage was hidden underneath.

'That?' Granda P pointed at his shoulder. 'Oh, don't worry about that, it's only a flesh wound, just a little scratch. The bullet only grazed the skin. It looks a lot worse than it is.' And that was as much time as Granda P wanted to spend talking about, or dealing with, his bullet wound!

'I don't think there's any point in trying their way out . . .' As Granda P stared round, a strong sense of urgency took possession of him, as well as his words. 'Oh my God! We're in trouble now. The tide's well in!'

There was no more thought given to Granda's wound as our stares were taken over by the level of the water below. Straight away we knew it was too high to allow us to return by the route we had taken in. Straight away, too, we realised there was no way out by climbing upwards. And just as suddenly it flashed on us there was no way out along the route the thieves and robbers had gone.

We were trapped!

21 STICKY PICKLES

Sometimes when you're in a sticky pickle, your mind concentrates to a degree it normally wouldn't or couldn't, and so you can come up with an answer, a solution to your problem. Mine did just that.

'The boat – we can use the robbers' boat to escape from here!'

Okay, it wasn't as if the answer wasn't there staring us all in the face, but I was first out with it. I felt quite pleased with myself.

'Excellent!' That was all Granda P had to say as he skipped off over the rocks and down from the perch we had safely ensconced ourselves on.

We were in luck: the ignition keys were still in the boat. But before we headed off, Granda P decided it would be a good idea if we switched the real gun box back into the boat. This was a lot easier said than done. For, try as we might and most certainly did, we didn't have the strength between us to even lift the other wooden box the robbers had placed in the boat.

Although none of us made reference to it directly, the main problem here was that Granda's right arm was far from functioning at its best. But we could wait from now until doomsday and we still wouldn't get to hear Granda P admit to there being anything wrong with him; not a chance!

Thankfully, Tom had a brainwave. He took out his penknife and proceeded to creak and squeak the lid of the box open, a little bit at a time, all the way along and around, and along and around, until there was enough of a peep to let Granda P get his fingers in under. Up and off and cast aside was the wooden lid of the large container, and there laughing up at us from inside were . . . stones and rocks – a lot of stones and rocks.

Granda laughed. 'Ha, ha! I might have known – there's no honour among thieves. Crooks who double-cross crooks! What is the world coming to?' Granda laughed some more and shook his head.

We lifted about half of the stones out and then we were able to remove the wooden box from the boat. This we duly refilled with the stones and replaced the lid after setting it down in the place of the other box with the guns which we just about managed to set in the boat. It was easy then to push the speedboat into the buoyancy of water needed before Granda P could start up the engine and ease us all out of the long, low, deep cave. And soon we were bounding and bouncing and crashing through the rising surge of waves washing in upon the island's jutty coast.

Granda had decided against running inland to retrieve the campervelle and then trying to catch up with the robbers. Time didn't allow for this, for by this stage we wouldn't have stood a chance of catching them, even from the air. Added to the time and distance factor was the fact that it was starting to get dark.

As usual, Granda P was correct in his interpretation of the way forward. So, instead of putting in at the first pier we saw, it was off to the nearest port to make contact with the police and let them take over the responsibility of catching the thieves.

At full pelt then, crashing through the crunching might and muscle of waves, we headed for the nearest, largest point of civilization to be lit up along the coastline. It was a calculated risk we were taking, but it was Granda P who had speculated on all the possibilities at our disposal, and he reckoned this was our best chance. According to Granda, it was unlikely the thieves would head inland to do a job, especially as big a job as this one sounded.

'Vermin tends to stick to its own run, to what it knows best. These boys won't stray far from the coast if they can help it.'

Hopefully Granda P was right; we were all banking on it.

We were thankful for the bright lights around the harbour as we pulled in, for the final stretch of our journey had been conducted in utter darkness. It was a very busy little port, judging by the number of vessels therein. Ours was the only activity on the water at this hour, though.

We managed to berth beside a slightly larger craft, which meant our boat was safely stashed, and it was easy enough for us to clamber over and onto the quay. "Welcome to St Peter Port" and "Bienvenue à la Port de

St Pierre" was the double message on a large sign along the harbour.

'Ah, we must have been on Sark. I wasn't sure whether we had landed on Herm or Sark. Now let's see how quickly we can find a police station.' As usual, Granda P had things sussed.

It wasn't yet the height of the tourist season, so the cafes and restaurants weren't packed with diners; and it wasn't yet late enough, so the streets weren't thronging with night revellers out on missions of enjoy. But it wasn't too long before we found someone who could point us in the right direction for the police station, and so off we headed at full pace, trying not to forget the street names included in the guidance.

St Peter Port is by no means a big place, and therefore it didn't take us long to find what we were looking for. But, for the first time so far in our adventure, our luck was out as on the front door of the police station was a notice stating its opening times. And it was closed.

We agreed with Granda P that there was little point in phoning a solitary policeman at home. After all, what could he do against seven hardened criminals, at least some of whom were armed? The answer to this didn't bear thinking about.

So, we were standing staring around ourselves, not knowing what our next move could or should be, when something very obvious, and not so obvious, caught my eye.

'That seems like a large bank for the size of the town . . .' I didn't know whether I was right or not, but

I had to say what was biting at the inside of my thinking. 'And look, there's a "To Let" sign next door. Do you think . . .'

I didn't have to state the obvious – it was right there in front of us. I let the rest of them work it out for themselves. It didn't take any sort of a detective genius to add these two together and come up with the best possibility we had. Therefore, without a word being said, the four of us were quick-stepping a direct route across the quiet street, and soon we were trying to stare into the interior of the "To Let" shop.

The glass on the big front window had been washed over with some sort of streaky white liquid and so there were only the occasional little slits of wavey gaps that we couldn't see very much through, or, in my case, that I couldn't see anything through at all. High, low and sideways we changed the challenge of the angle of our peep in an effort to see what wasn't there to see, or so I thought.

'I think I can see something . . .' No one else seemed to pick up on what Siobhan had said. 'I did. I saw a light flash inside, over there. You must have seen it! Did anyone see it?'

The want in Siobhan's voice made me wish I had seen it, seen something, seen anything, so that I could agree with her, so that we would be on the right tracks. But something made me look away, the sound of something different.

'Yeah, I thought I saw something, too. It could have been a light.' Tom didn't sound so sure, yet it was enough to make me turn my head away from the street that had momentarily attracted my attentions.

'Run!'

As tyres screeched to a halt on the road behind, the shop door flung open from inside and all I could do was catch a sideways glance of Monsieur Henri hurrying out with a heavy rucksack slung over his shoulder. More crunchy footsteps followed immediately after, but I didn't get a chance to look at these – I was too busy being flung through the air in the opposite direction, alongside Tom.

Just in the nick of time, Granda P must have added the same two and two together and come up with the fact that we were in the right place but at the wrong time. His automatic reaction was to catch hold of the two closest to him and fling them to safety.

'Stop them!' The second robber out after Monsieur Henri was the bearded Harry guy and his shout alerted the gang to the danger of the moment.

It all happened in a flash. After throwing Tom and my dumbfounded self out of the way to safety, Granda P swung round to grab Siobhan but he was a split second too late. Monsieur Henri was first to react. He grabbed Siobhan and dragged her with him as he dived into the back of the waiting van. As the rest of the band of robbers hurried out of the shop, their booty stashed in rucksacks over their shoulders, there were a couple of guns pointed in our direction.

Not another word was shouted by the robbers, not a sound was needed to be sent in our direction. The smiles on their ugly faces indicated who was in control of the situation. Granda P had no option but to stand with his arms high in the air while Tom and my scared self stood frozen to the spot.

It was all over in a matter of seconds. The getaway van screeched off down the street, round the corner and out of sight, with our sis in it, kidnapped by a gang of low-down, no-good, cowardly, well armed thieves and robbers.

We stood there mesmerised, hypnotised, spell-bound, and magnetised to the spot. Inside our stupefied selves we were petrified, paralysed by fear, not alone for ourselves, but mostly for Siobhan, our darling sis now stolen away from us by that grotesque gang of gangsters. It felt as if our bodies had been turned to stone, but only momentarily, until reality began to seep in. This was definitely another sticky pickle.

It happened so quickly, like a flash of lightening, for then they were gone and I just wanted to fall down and cry and wail and bemoan Siobhan's loss and the desperate danger she was in. I didn't get a chance to. I didn't get a chance to dwell on what was lost and gone because a push on the shoulder, one each for Tom and my miserable self, sent us running off, playing catch-up with Granda.

'Come on, back to the boat! If we hurry, we'll make it back to their lair before them. They'll never suspect we know where they're going, and Siobhan won't say anything, will she?' Granda was pounding off ahead of Tom and my quickening self.

'Not a chance. Siobhan won't give the game away.'

I was glad Tom answered; I didn't think I would have been able to, so puffed was I with worry and thought, not to mention the speed we were haring back down to the boat at.

I don't know where Granda P got all his energy from. I don't know where a man his age got his speed from, because neither Tom nor my slackening self had the slightest chance of catching up with him. So, by the time we jumped aboard, the engine was started, Granda P had cast off, and it was all systems go for us.

On the journey back to the island, there was no room for chat or talk about what had happened, not to mention what was going to happen. Our minds were rampant with a single, solitary thought. We kept lookout as best we could lest we hit any rocks. Granda had the speedboat pounding the waves at full throttle, and he was cutting it fine, hugging the shortest route back, which was the one closest to shore, so we could have been splattered against an outcrop of rock at any moment.

We didn't care. There was only one consideration in our minds, and it was Siobhan and how we were ever going to manage to rescue her.

The darkness of the night as we powered across a lonely stretch of water might under normal circumstances have been very scary, but not tonight. The reflection of light off the moon offered just about enough illumination for us to see how closely Granda P was cutting the angle of his attack. The ever-diminishing distance of sea between us and our target produced an ever-increasing level of worry, with the thought that our luck wouldn't last the distance.

Bumpety, bumpety, bumpety, bump. At times it felt like we were flying, so high were we bouncing off the skim of the water, but this only lasted until we landed back down with a smash. Very quickly were the embracing lights of St Peter Port left behind in the darkness of distance, leaving us nothing but a scant measure of moonlight and the grace of God's goodwill to steer us safely on our way.

But, as fortune favours the brave, the boat made it back in one piece with us in it. The relief of stepping back onto slippery rocks was magnificent and I was about to tie the boat up to a rock when Granda P stopped me. He took the rope from my hands and flung it into the water.

'It can find its own destiny. At least the boat and the weapons won't be here for their use if they do escape us.'

With a shove from his sole, the speedboat was released to its fate. Once again, Granda P was right with his quick thinking. We were all very glad to see the end of so many guns. At least now they were well out of the reach of the criminal minds who would only do harm with them.

Then we stole back to the cave. It didn't matter that we were unable to get in: we could see and hear from outside there was definitely nothing happening inside. We waited and waited, but nobody returned to the cave. Not another sound did we hear except the constant wash of waves upon the jut of rocks amid the musical lap and slap of water against the unevennesses of rock all around. And so the tide was well on the wane by the time we stirred our tired selves from the hiding positions we were hunkered in.

'We'd best find our way back to the campervelle and go in search of your poor sister.'

There was no great volume to Granda's tone, and so it wasn't difficult to determine how, in the light of Siobhan not being with us, he was feeling. Exactly the same level of despondency was apparent in Tom and my disconsolate self.

It was slippery work finding our way back out from the cave and round to where we had earlier stashed the wagen, or so we thought. We looked everywhere but, try as we might, we could not locate it in the clouded darkness.

Suddenly a shout: 'There it is!' Granda's military-type night-vision experience clearly paid off. The wagen was outlined in the distance as the moon momentarily pierced its sheathing shroud.

However, we didn't go straight to it. Instead, we skirted around the vicinity of the campervelle, all the time watching, looking and listening as best we could, in case there was anything untoward lying in wait for us. As far as we could determine, there was no one about. So, with Granda P taking the lead, we very cautiously moved in on it.

'The two of you come round this side. Stand up on the footplate here and cover as much of the glass area as you possibly can with yourselves. The light's going to go on as soon as I unlock the door.' Granda's whispered instructions sounded wonderfully through the deadness of the night.

We did as we were told, to the best of our ability, and only a few slats of light escaped the wrap of our bodies.

In less than a split second, Granda P had nobbled the light so it would know better than to come on when he didn't want it to in future.

Then we were inside sitting: Tom in the front, me in the back, and Granda P driving slowly, carefully, lightlessly, along the narrow crackle of so much gravel under tread. I don't know what speed we were doing – I know it never seems as fast in the back as it does in the front – but we didn't seem to be putting much distance between ourselves and behind.

I had to stop my negative thoughts. I had to think positively. At least we were moving. At least we were doing something positive, even if it was only at around ten miles per hour. Then, as we rounded another tight turn in the track, we caught sight of a house.

'Right, we'll park her up here.' Granda had carefully and quietly guided the wagen into a reversed position still some way from the house, ready for a quick getaway if needed. Once safely parked, he began rummaging behind the back seats.

'This is an old machine I picked up for free from a hospital. Can you believe they were actually going to dump it? Amazing!'

As Granda P rattled on, he leant over the back row of seats and set up some machine that he had stashed in the boot. It had a lot of buttons and knobs on the base and a part that reached up like an arm but with a hollow end piece instead of a hand. This part Granda P pointed out the back window and off in the direction of the house. There was also a small screen attached onto it, which obviously wasn't part of the machine but looked like one of Granda's homemade inventions.

'They've no respect for quality these days,' Granda continued to no one in particular. 'They're obsessed with the latest in gimmickry and gadgetry – and the most expensive, of course. It's of no consequence to their fleeting minds that this has worked perfectly well for a decade or more. Oh no, out with the old, in with the new, that's the modern motto.'

Tom and my unbelieving self both regarded this contraption in the same way: we would be amazed if it worked at all, whatever it was. But we said nothing and let Granda P get on with whatever it was he had to do. After the complication of arrangements before he could begin, Granda P finally plugged his strange appliance into the cigar lighter in the front and then flicked a switch.

'It'll take a few moments to get warmed up. Very sore on the battery this is; you'll have to remind me to recharge it when we get home. I wouldn't want her to break down on our way out for a bottle of milk, which we're always running out of recently, certainly not anything as important as that!'

Granda smiled at us. It wasn't a very deep smile but it was enough to keep us in hope. This was the only time Granda P took his eyes off the machine or his fingers off blending buttons round to re-correct their positioning.

'Right! We're ready now. Watch this!'

The machine made a nice mixture of buzzing noises, and black and white fuzzy-type images or shapes appeared and disappeared on the TV screen as Granda P angled the cup-shaped end piece around. Back and forth, back and forth, he moved this part of his gadget before flicking the mains switch and thus killing off its life-sustaining feed of electricity.

'Nobody there. Right, off to the next house.'

Granda threw himself round and a couple of crouched paces landed him back in the driver's seat. From our silence it must have been obvious that we hadn't a clue what was going on, for we really didn't have a notion what Granda P was working at.

'Have you not worked it out yet?' His question came at us like a bolt of lightening through the darkness, blinding us to the little bit of seeing we already had. Not a word, not an utterance, not a solitary sound was articulated by either Tom or my silent self. We hadn't a clue what was what, not to mention what wasn't what.

'It's an X-ray machine!'

My suspicions were confirmed. I thought it might be, thought it must be, because I couldn't think of what else it could be. But I didn't like to say. I wasn't sure so I kept schtum because I didn't want to show my ignorance. I didn't want to appear stupid. I didn't want it to appear I knew nothing at all about . . .

'Aren't X-rays dangerous?'

I don't know why I asked. Well, I *do* know why. I asked because it was all that was in my head, it was all I could think of; but I still don't know why I went ahead and blabbered out the first silly notion that took hold of me. And Tom, of course, had the good sense to keep his trap firmly shut.

'Oh, don't listen to the prattle of all the nonsense providers the world has to offer: they'll wear you out and leave you with nothing to do and, more importantly, nothing done. A little bit of everything in this life will not do you enough harm to notice.'

Thankfully, Granda's tone wasn't dismissive of me. He was getting his old optimistic self back into gear.

Unfortunately, this increase in optimism wasn't enough to ward off the flood of pessimism we felt when the second house registered a blank on the screen, too. Onward we went, not dwelling on this disappointment for even a moment and most definitely not daring to mention what we would, or could, or couldn't do if the other houses turned out to be empty as well.

As Granda P set up his home-improved X-ray machine for the third time, we all held our breath. Then, as if by magic, bony figures of moving persons appeared on the screen in front of us. Success, at last!

Very carefully, Granda P moved his scope back and forth, back and forth, until we all agreed there were eight figures in the house. One of these eight, in an upstairs room, didn't have use of arms or legs: it had to be Siobhan. She was tied to a chair in a room at the front of the house and there was a pile of bones sitting picking and poking between his eyeballs and his trap, just outside this room. However, he most definitely had a gun in his lap. Poor Siobhan!

'Right,' whispered Granda P, 'listen up. We have to get Siobhan out. And quickly, before they try to move her again or use her as a hostage. This is what we are going to do.' And with that, Granda P outlined his daring rescue plan.

22 SIOBHAN'S GREAT RESCUE

After memorising the positions of all the robbers around the house as best we could, we set to with our plan.

First of all, Tom sneaked up to the front door with a good length of rope, tied one end onto the front door handle, back-tracked as quickly and quietly as he possibly could and then tied the other end securely onto a wall pillar not too far away. Tom sidled back down along a hedge and into the wagen. His eyes were flashing with the brilliance of the moment, for, even in the darkness of our surrounds, I could feel his excitement burst in upon us. But all that was pouring through my mind was my imminent role in the Great Rescue.

As Granda P eased the campervelle out and away from the house, my heart was pounding ever stronger as the balloon went up and we began to take off up, up, up, into the lightness of dark air all around. My adrenalin pump was working on full throttle as we floated quietly over toward the house and around to the targeted front window. Then, as I noiselessly slid the side door open and Tom moved over and held it for me, I eased myself forward as best I could, clutching onto whatever came to hand.

Closer, closer, nearer, nearer, Granda P positioned the wagen right up against the window of the room Siobhan was bound and locked in. I took out my penknife, opened its blade, and held it in the bite of my front teeth, ready for action.

As calmly as I could, I leant forward beyond the full stretch of my frame. Now I was committed, now I had no choice but to continue, now there was no going back. My balance was compromised as I half held onto, half tugged, at the wooden frame of the window. There was no shift in it. It refused to budge. Try as I might, there was no way this window was going to open under the authority of my determination.

I released the penknife from the grip of my teeth, placed it carefully in between where the sash windows met, flicked the latch open, and gently glided the lower half of the frame up enough to slide my body inside. In the faintness of light spilling into the room, I caught the beauty of Siobhan's eyes light up, bound and gagged as she was. I smiled back my joy.

Carefully, without even the hint of a noise, I soft-stepped over and cut the rope binding Siobhan's hands and feet behind the chair. As soon as she released her gag, we hugged. I don't remember when we last hugged. It was certainly a long time ago. But there was nothing else we could do, we just had to hug – even though this wasn't included in my allotted rescue role.

While sis exited by the window, straight into the wagen with Tom's help, I positioned her chair up against the door handle. They'd be a long time trying to shift that in. No sooner was I back inside the safety and warmth of the campervelle, enjoying the sheer luxury of us all being together again, than Granda P had us manoeuvred off and away from the house. But then he landed not too far down the front garden.

'I've had an idea. This'll not take long. I'll be straight back, hopefully!' With this, Granda P reached down and lifted out a cylinder of something plus a length of tubing from under the front seat. As he turned to go, I just caught the snatch of writing on the cylinder: nitrous oxide, N_2O. He must have had all kinds of everything in this wagen. And I felt sick at the thought of us safely stashed inside the wagen while Granda headed off, alone, back up toward the lion's den.

In the enormity of hours that probably didn't amount to much more than a couple of minutes, the three of us chatted probably a lot more than we had done in the previous couple of months.

It was good, it was great, it was the most magnificent of feelings being reunited with the ones you love. Although we wouldn't actually say this, we couldn't help but show it to each other, knowing fine rightly inside our heads that as soon as the pressure of present fear was off us, we would probably revert to type and fall into the old way of being normal and horrid toward one another.

For now, though, Granda P was missing. For the massive time delay ticking through each one of the over-expanded seconds, he still wasn't back with us. What should we do? What could we do? Should we wait for him and risk us all getting caught? Should we stay or should we follow that nagging, biting sensation inside, take to our heels and run for our lives?

We didn't have long to discuss this. We didn't need

long to discuss it because we had thought of nothing else ourselves and we could see in our looks, we could feel in the gut instinct inside, that this was one chance too many, it was an unnecessary risk. And then, just when we were ready to act on the impulse thus far ignored, it was too late!

'Hahahahahahahaggghhh!'

The laughscream swallowed up the whole night, consuming the complete blanket of darkness we were steeped in. It was human in its origin. It was loud. It was enough to make every hair on your head extend beyond its fullest extension with fear.

'What was that?'

'Where was that?'

'Who was that?'

We couldn't move. We just sat there in a helpless, scarebound suspension of our petrified selves until—

'Hahahahahahahaggghhh!'

Our eyes nearly popped out of their sockets when we heard it again. This time, however, it was followed by another and another and another; high-pitched blasts of mirthful, farcical hilarity that started up slowly and picked up a rhythm and motion all its own in time.

'I hope they haven't caught Granda and are deriving pleasure from torturing him!'

I hadn't thought of it this way. I hadn't thought of it the way sis's mind worked.

'No, no, I don't think so . . . That's laughter, uncontrollable, side-splitting chuckings of the funnies coming out of the house: the N_2O must be working!' I breathed a heavy sigh of relief through my determination. We all eased the strangle of fear from our frozen frames. But not for long!

We heard a noise at the side of the wagen. We caught a glimpse of the side of a head that turned round to look back toward the house. Was it that French thug, Monsieur Henri, waiting on his band of ne'er-do-wells to catch up with him before launching into an attack on us?

Whatever way darkness held cover over that side of the campervelle, it was impossible to distinguish exactly who was who. I don't mind admitting it – I've never been so scared in my whole life as I was during those frozen few seconds that lasted for hours. The three of us were beside ourselves with fear.

Then the body turned round. The head was pointing in our direction. The face was staring right into our belong. The man came right over to the driver's door and pulled on the handle – he was trying to get in!

'Come on! Hurry up! Open up!'

It was Granda! As a very basic precaution, I had snibbed the driver's door locked as soon as he had left. As the fear drained from within us, I immediately freed the lock and in jumped Granda. He quickly started up the engine, and we were out of there post-haste. Up, up, up into the air we headed, away from the house full of laughing thieves, and not a single, solitary word was sounded between the lot of us.

I think it must have been the conscious, internal registering of relief that left us unable to speak, that left us entering back into the normal world of being together again and feeling at one within ourselves as well as with each other. In fact, it wasn't until we were well away from there and had caught sight of the bright lights of St Peter Port that a giggle of laughter caught hold of us and grew and grew as we flew and flew.

In the end up, there were three pairs of young cheeks soaking wet with the constant flow of absurd tears down them. In all honesty, we knew that a large measure of what was flowing from us was in the form of a safety valve, helping all our recent fear and distress escape from inside. From the measure of Granda sitting there, fully in control of the wheel of the wagen, I knew to look at him he was fearless of anything past, present or to come.

'We'll put her down in the town centre. That should cause a bit of a stir. At least then we should attract some attention and someone might have the good sense to call the police.' There was ease in Granda's tone again, ease that had probably come from the alleviation of annoyance, and, I suppose, relief we were all at our own convenience again.

Well, someone must have seen us coming from a long way out, or perhaps we had shown up on their defence system's radar scanners – or possibly not. Whatever the way of it, as soon as we touched down, a whole heap of police, many with guns and rifles aimed in our direction, surrounded the campervelle. It looked like we had jumped out of the frying pan and into the fire!

'Come out with your hands in the air. Lay down your weapons. We have you surrounded. You cannot escape.'

I don't know what planet the policeman with the loudhailer was from; it certainly wasn't anywhere near our galaxy. But his squeaky voice sounded very much like he had been at the helium, too, for his tea.

'I wonder what odds I would get on that one.'

This was all Granda said before smiling back at us as he stepped out of the wagen. Although he kept his hands above his head, Granda proceeded to ignore all other warning shouts as he quick-stepped over to the commander with the loudhailer, who by now was standing behind two more robustly-sized policemen.

Soon, guns were lowered and policemen and policewomen began to mill around the wagen. We were safe! Granda had obviously satisfied them as to our innocence in all matters illegal. Then he was back over with us, along with the commander and a few other officers, and it was smiles all round as we sat chatting with all the doors open.

'The police are out in force because of the bank robbery. I'll go with them to show exactly where is what and who is why, if you know what I mean.' Granda smiled a great big, happy smile.

Siobhan, of course, jumped out and hugged him. 'Please be careful, Granda.' And then she looked up at the police commander. 'Take good care of my granda, won't you? He's the only one we've got. And make sure you treat his shoulder. He was shot, you know.'

If sis kept this up, she'd have us all in floods of tears again, only of the soppy-soppy variety this time.

'Of course I will. We'll get his wound sorted and Sergeant Lewis here will take you to our best hotel. I'm sure you're all very tired.'

It definitely wasn't the loudhailer's fault. It clearly was the police commander's voice that held a genuine squeegee mix of a squeak, a squawk and a squeal.

The three of us had to muster our whole determination so as not to laugh. Of course we wanted to say 'No'. Of course we wanted to say we were going with Granda, we were a team and we wouldn't let one go without all going. 'All for fun and fun for all!' as Granda liked to say.

But all at once, exhaustion decided it for us. It was late, very late. In our minds we were glad we had come to the end of a long and extremely exhausting day. But physically, it felt as if, having pulled the plug on all the terror and trepidation, all the apprehension and anxiety, all the dire, dreadful distress, that they had been replaced with a slumberous, hypnotic, sleep-inducing state. We might well have been back to our old confident selves, but it was impossible to say because we were so, so sleepy.

And the thought of hotel, bed, sleep, bath, food, warmth, shelter – well, it all came together and left us so yearning for the joy of it all we found we couldn't resist, no matter how much we may have wanted to. So, we did as we were told.

Therefore, before we knew it, we were falling into the soft, inviting, comforting warmth of delectably snuggly beds with deliciously fresh sheets wrapping us up in sleep.

What a day!

23 BOOM! BANG! WHOOSH!

When we woke up, there was lightness and brightness streaming in through the windows and Granda was standing there, smiling brilliantly.

'I've had your breakfasts brought up to you. Eat what you want or eat everything you want, and then we can get going. If I didn't waken you we'd have to spend another night here.'

Granda had already hooked the curtains into the hold of their tie-backs. Now I could see it, this really was a gorgeous big room, grandeur beyond our wildest expectations! In fact, it wasn't a room, it was a suite. They must have planted us in the grandest suite, in the poshest hotel, on the island.

The focus of my attention was then taken by my study of the face of the wristband attached to my left arm. I couldn't believe what it was telling me. I couldn't believe what I was seeing.

'It's three o'clock in the afternoon! I've never lain on so long in my whole life; none of us have. I'd love to see

Momsie's face if she knew we had a lie-in until three o'clock in the afternoon!' I felt so cheered inside myself, I couldn't help but smile.

'This will definitely go down in family history as the longest lie-in ever.' I think Tom had more to say on the matter but his mouth was overcome by the need to show off his tonsils, so deep was his yawn. The stretch of his arms was so wide that he fell back upon the delightful rescue of his pillows.

I must have momentarily dozed off, and when I looked over at Siobhan in her bed, and Tom in his bed, I noticed they weren't saying anything because they weren't able to, so busy were they tucking into what looked like breakfast, lunch and dinner all rolled onto one big tray.

Orange juice and tea and milk, surrounded by cereals of every crunchy sort. Bread and rolls and toast and little squares of butter, and little pots of marmalade, and littler pots of jam. And then a big dinner plate. And on this dinner plate sat two fried eggs, three sausages, four rashers of bacon, mushrooms by the plenty, beans by the uncountable, hash browns, potato bread, scrambled egg, and that's all I can remember. And guess what? We ate the lot!

After freshening up in a bathroom bigger than any of our bedrooms at home, we were all standing in the hotel foyer ready to depart about half an hour later. There wasn't a flurry of smiles to see us off. I was disappointed with this. I think we all were. But there was a police commander, minus his loudhailer, of course. He had brought along a couple of colleagues, one male and one female, to say goodbye. There was no speech, no words of thanks, just a simple:

'We'll be in touch.'

Granda nodded his agreement to this, and so we were off, driving this time, off to catch the ferry which left in less than an hour. We were all so busy with the thought of heading back homewards that none of us thought to ask the obvious. And so we didn't.

In fact, it wasn't until we were settled into the stay of the queue to board the ferry that we could begin to focus in on what was past, as well as what was to come. By this stage, our stomachs had had a chance to settle and we had the capacity to think of something other than what to do when our bellies burst open!

'Did they all come quietly or did they put up a fight, or had they laughed themselves silly by the time the police caught them?'

As soon as Tom asked his question, we were all dying to know. We simply had to hear how Granda and the police had got on with the capture of the gasified gangsters and raucous robbers. We had our eyes, our minds, our ears, and all parts of our conscious selves on a high state of alert ready to absorb every minute detail Granda was about to educate our interest with.

'Nothing to it, really.'

Nothing to it, really? Of course there was. There was plenty to it. There was every move, every order, every shadow, every rip, every click of a twig snapping underfoot; in fact, every everything that might have been something totally different. Every shout, every warning, every knock, every kick and thump, every dash, every grab, every 'You're under arrest', every clack of handcuffs locking hands behind thievish backs. Every 'Take them away, constable, and throw them in jail!'

We wanted every nuance of every detail. We needed every peculiar aspect of every particular moment. And we demanded it all be related back to us now and retold with all the gusto befitting a character of Granda's standing.

Right at that moment, at that precise point in the history of all the thousands of years of time, the Zoom-Zang-Alang pitching up from the engine cut out. Something had caused it to stall. But, perhaps more to the point, this caused Granda to stall and refrain from filling our minds with every perfect detail of the capture of seven criminals.

With that, the front passenger door abruptly opened and into the wagen pushed the burly figure and bearded face of Harry — one of the robbers from back home, and one of the seven deadly thieves from here. Siobhan was shoved off her seat and landed in between Tom and my astonished self.

'Act as if everything is okay. If anyone does or says anything wrong, the old geezer gets it!'

He didn't look his best, and he certainly didn't sound too happy. He had his right hand in his jacket pocket and something inside this was definitely pointing in Granda's direction. The important little details in life didn't appear to have been going this robber's way. It was impossible to state categorically whether or not he had a gun in his pocket. We couldn't risk calling his bluff in case it wasn't only a finger he was threatening us with. There was no way any of us were prepared to risk that.

'Sorry, but I was about to tell you . . .'

At this, the thief pushed his pointed pocket out further, and we caught the sad, worried state of Granda's face reflected in the rear-view mirror.

'One of them managed to escape. It must be this one.' There was more than just a hint of a derisory smile in Granda's look, and he finished this off with a wink.

I was surprised. We all were, for this wasn't exactly the kind of situation that warranted showing off your happy side. We sat numbfounded, struck dumb, too, by the threatening presence in the front passenger seat.

'Shift it! The rest of the line has moved off. Don't try drawing attention to us by holding up the rest of the queue!'

There was real, tough, bullying menace in every aspect of our unwanted guest's demeanour.

'We'd better see if she's going to start, then, hadn't we?'

With his look, as well as his words, as well as his body language, Granda showed he would stand up to anyone. He wouldn't be cowed into submission by the coarse threats of a sinister ruffian, no matter what might be pointing from his pocket. With a quick flick of the ignition key, the engine was up and running again and Granda P made to move off. He stopped suddenly and stared over at the robber.

'You'd better put your seatbelt on, unless you want the police to stop us.'

Begrudgingly, the thief did as he was told, and soon we were trundling along over the rough concrete surface heading toward the massive opening at the back of the ferry. Just then, Granda made to scratch an itch on his ankle and flicked a switch hidden under his seat.

BOOM! BANG! WHOOSH!

Up shot the robber's seat, with him attached to it, up through the emergency escape hatch in the roof. Off he soared, up, up, up, into the air high above; before a small parachute opened to bring him safely back down to earth, without too much of a thud.

'What do you reckon? Fifty feet? Sixty, maybe?' Granda's eyes had grown. They were now almost the size of two footballs with this fantastic feat of exciting achievement.

'Oh, at least sixty . . . even seventy . . . maybe more!'

Siobhan was the only one of the three of us who could speak. Tom's jaw looked exactly the same as mine, as if the tendons had been snapped and we were left with this wide, yawning, enormous gap between our noses and our dropped chins.

By now, too, a small crowd of onlookers had gathered and they were clapping and cheering, and amongst their number stood two policemen, plus an ever-growing straggle of security personnel.

'Arrest that man, he's . . .'

We didn't hear the remainder of what Granda said, but we didn't need to hear it, for we knew in essence what it amounted to. Anyway, with the velocity of his landing on the reinforced concrete, I think the robber was glad of the help of the two policemen as they arrested, handcuffed, and hobbled him away.

By now, too, the bevy of bemused onlookers had swallowed the disbelief of all they had seen, and probably mentally noted this as the highlight of their holiday, as they all made their way back to their places in the queue.

Meanwhile, despite a few honks from the line-up of vehicles behind, Granda wasn't going anywhere without his beloved, rocket-propelled front seat, and so Tom and my laughing self jumped out and helped him lift it in.

'How many more surprises does the campervelle

have?' Perhaps Tom was seeking an answer to an impossible question. Perhaps there is, perhaps there isn't, an impossible answer to an impossible question.

'It's been so long since I installed some of them, I can hardly remember myself; but memory won't let you down when you need it.' Here, Granda appeared to have a thought stuck at the forefront of his mind. Not for long, though – he gave his head a shake and opened his eyes wide. 'That rocket is a bit noisy but there's no doubt it does its job of work. I'm not so sure about the landing, though: I think the parachute might need an extra inch or three!'

The wryness of Granda's grin contorted my own thoughts so that I didn't know what to make of what he had said, or indeed, what to make of my own feelings.

'I reckon we could have done with three or four inches *off* it; then he might have got the landing he deserved!' A cheeky face held the measure of Siobhan's thoughts and, of us all, she had good reason to feel this way, given that she was the only one who managed to get herself kidnapped.

'Well, you now know where the ejection lever is. You just have to make sure the wagen is in motion when you flick it. Everything else you'll find out in good time, or as soon as I remember.'

Granda crunched her into first gear, and with a glorious burst of Zoom-Zang-Alang, we headed up the ramp and into the cavernous hold of the ferry.

'That's enough excitement to last till we get home!'

It was Granda who said it, but it was all of us who

thought it. We certainly had more than our quota of heart-enhancing thrills of late, enough perhaps until the three of us began to make wrinkles of our own.

So, for most of the journey back to our great mass of land, we did nothing more than sit contentedly and quietly on deck, staring out to sea, to see what we could see. That great, endless looking expanse of water was perfect for absorbing our intentions and leaving us with nothing to think about except our own thoughts, nothing to worry us except what had happened.

It's important sometimes, just before or just after times of crisis, chaos or difference, to close your mind to all outside interference, especially primary intentions. And just do nothing. Perfect!

We'd had a truly excellent adventure. And now it was time for home.

When we three excited but exhausted adventurers returned safely home again on the train, we were bursting to tell Momsie and Dad all about our event-filled trip. But we felt guilty that we had not phoned home to find out what had transpired with Merlin's Magical Chest Enhancers and Momsie's newspaper exposé, so we said little and listened a lot.

Much to our collective relief, it turned out that the article had been spiked and replaced by a breaking story about some famous international footballer: "Silver Spheres Plays Away From Home" – something I thought footballers did every fortnight anyway as part of their contract.

The great news turned to magnificent when, instead of the expected front-page "Merlin's Magical Chest Enhancers – All Revealed" article and accompanying embarrassing photo, the paper ran a lengthy piece on Momsie's chocolate porridge in the Women's Magazine supplement. Famous celebrity chef Gary Sadmoron had been asked to try it out by the appreciative journalist who had taken some home with him and, lo and behold, his article, "I ***** Love Momsie's Chocolate Porridge!", had started the phone ringing off the hook with media enquiries and major store-chain orders.

So, Dad had graciously set aside his own Merlin invention and had secured a fabtastic exclusive deal with multi-national company Deus Ex Machina Food Stuffs to produce and globally market Momsie'e unique breakfast cereal. Which meant that, thanks to Momsie's natural kindness and her secret recipe for chocolate porridge, surprisingly and wonderfully and incredibly – we were:

RICH!!

We congratulated them both, over and over and over, and cheered and whooped and laughed till the wee small hours. We phoned Granda who joined in with his own gleeful gladness and promises to visit soon to continue the celebrations.

And together we three siblings secretly shared the same magical thought:

What amazing adventures lay ahead of us, now that the world was ours to explore and enjoy!

THE END